School of of Scares

A Field Park Horror Novel

D1528374

Christina Hagmann

School of Scares

A Field Park Horror Novel

Copyright © 2022 by Christina Hagmann

All rights reserved.

Cover Art by JOELEE ART

ISBN 979-8-7982-1710-6

www.christinahagmann.com

RWD Publishing

Chapter 1

A note slid over from the other side of the table. I opened it. The words were scrawled in yellow crayon. "I love you."

I folded the note and crushed it in my hand before looking over my shoulder to see if anyone was watching. Jay, who sat one row over and one table back, turned and looked. She must have seen the deer in headlights look on my face because her eyebrows creased in confusion. She mouthed, "What?"

I turned back around, but didn't look at him. He knew I had a boyfriend. Why was he doing this to me?

Mr. Zimbo, my English teacher, continued to drone on about Shakespeare, but the paper in my hand drowned out his words. I knew he was talking about Othello, the tragic hero, and the cultural context of the play. We wouldn't be reading it until next year, but I'd just seen the new movie with Josh Hartnett based on the play. I thought it was a basketball movie. Little did I know, my date night would become a lesson in literature.

I glanced at my hand, and then I dared to glance at Zach from the corner of my eye. He had the audacity to stare straight at me and grace me with one of his full tooth grins. Closing my eyes, I shook my head. I wished I could say this was the only time this happened, but since I'd grown breasts, more of my male friends thought that the reason I talked to them was that I wanted to date them. It was as though they forgot we were friends first. But not Zach. I'd never thought Zach would do this to me.

"Sam!" I heard someone hiss from a nearby desk. I looked over to see my best friend Jay holding a note in her hand. At first, I was confused, thinking someone had passed her a love note. She recognized my confusion and waved her note in the air. "It's tonight." She gave me a nod.

Next to me, Zach let out a huff of air. I turned and faced him.

"What?" I asked.

"You didn't know?" He nodded to Jay. "Tonight is Freshmeat Night."

I studied his face, and a realization dawned on me. "Wait. Is that why you gave me the note? Did you think you'd hook up with me tonight?" I shook my head in disgust. "Not a chance. Besides, you know I have a boyfriend." I knew that wasn't what the note was about, but it was easier to be angry than to consider the implications and complications of such a declaration from Zach, who'd been my best friend since second grade.

"Sam, you've known me long enough to know it wasn't about that. I care about you." He moved his hand closer to me. "And I know you care about me, too. That's why you called." I stared at his hand, thinking about my phone call to him last night. We talked until three in the morning. My parents would have murdered me if they knew I was up that late.

I opened my mouth to speak, but a yardstick smacked down on the table in between us.

"Am I interrupting you?" Mr. Zimbo asked, leaning close to my face and breathing coffee and onions into my nose.

Zach said, "No, sir. Sam was just helping me find the page I'm supposed to be on." He tipped his head toward me. "See?" He pointed to the open book.

"Tut, tut, Zachary. Don't you know there is no talking in class? And I saw what happened before with that note." He ignored Zach and leaned closer to me. "You seem so innocent, Samantha, but you can be just as bad as these boys can."

I kept a straight face as Mr. Zimbo walked back to the front of the room and paced back and forth. I took a deep breath, knowing what this meant. He was about to give a long lecture about something that had nothing to do with Shakespeare.

"Well, Mr. Markan, if you'd been paying attention in the first place, rather than making eyes at Ms. Elliot, then you wouldn't have needed her help." He slapped the yardstick in his free hand.

I stole a glance at Zach, trying to recall if he ever made eyes at me.

"Now, as I was saying." He continued to pace the front of the room. "Mr. Markan, I put you by Ms. Elliot because I thought then you wouldn't continue walking across the room to talk to her. It seems that my plan has backfired." I looked again out of the corner of my eye and saw a hint of red on Zach's cheek. I was sure mine looked the same.

"No matter where Ms. Elliot is seated, she is the flame, and you are the moth."

"Roadhouse!" someone called from the back of the room, and the class erupted in laughter. I let go of the breath I was holding now that all eyes weren't on us.

Mr. Zimbo spun on his heels. "Mr. Barrington, I suggest you keep your comments to yourself unless you want my full attention."

"Sorry, Mr. Zimbo. I was talking about Sam." Bear grinned at me, and I rolled my eyes in return.

"I don't care what you were talking about. I only care that your lips were moving when they shouldn't be." Mr. Zimbo turned and walked back up to the chalkboard.

"But, Sam Elliot? Roadhouse? Get it?" He continued to talk as Mr. Zimbo wrote a few words on the board.

I turned and gave Bear the finger. He laughed, and Jay giggled from somewhere behind me. Bear leaned close to Kate, his tablemate, and whispered something that made her face turn bright red. He looked back at me and raised an eyebrow. I shook my head in disgust and turned back.

Mr. Zimbo didn't face the class. "Oh, I get it, Barrington. Roadhouse, the 1989 film starring Patrick Swayze and the actor Sam Elliott. I get it indeed. I just don't think it is particularly clever."

"Thank you," I responded before turning back and making a face at Barrington.

"Zip it, Ms. Elliot. I'm trying to teach a class." He pressed his chalk to the board and scratched in the reading assignment for the weekend. He tossed the chalk on the ledge and turned to face the class.

I raised my hand. "Um, Mr. Zimbo?"

"What is it, Ms. Elliot?"

"Um, I prefer to be called Roadhouse, sir." The class erupted in laughter, and Mr. Zimbro rolled his eyes at me.

Zach's elbow connected with mine, and when I looked at him, his hand was over his mouth, and his shoulders shook with laughter.

"Be gone. You are all useless to me at this point. Do the reading assignment and be safe this weekend." He waved his arms at us, dismissing us, before hobbling over to his desk. He shot me a dirty look and sat in his chair, paging through an old paperback book.

The class let out another round of laughter. Mr. Zimbo was a cranky old man, but he was funny. Plus, he always handled any discipline with public humiliation, which made us all admire him.

Barrington pushed his way past me so he could walk with Zach. I watched as Zach slid his yellow crayon into his back pocket. My eyes traveled up just as he was looking over his shoulder. He raised an eyebrow at me, and I knew what he was thinking. A hint of a grin appeared on his face as he looked ahead. I chastised myself as Jay saddled up to me in the hallway.

"Um, what was that all about?" she asked, nudging me as she shifted her books into her other arm.

"Nothing," I mumbled, rolling the note smaller into my hand so she wouldn't see it. We followed the wave of students making their way from the back hallway to the locker bays, all near the cafeteria.

She unfolded her note with her free hand. "It's Fresh-meat Night tonight." She scowled at me.

"What? We knew it was coming soon." I shrugged and shoved the note in my pocket while trying not to drop my book and binder.

"Yeah, but why this weekend? I wanted to go out tonight." She looked down at her shoes and kicked a pencil across the floor.

"I know, but there are worse ways to spend a Friday night. Plus, it's one step closer to being part of the team."

She muttered something under her breath.

"What?" I had no idea what she said.

"Nothing... it's one step closer. I just wish it could be different for once, ya know?" She gathered her books closer to her chest and squinted down the hallway.

I had to admit I saw where she was coming from. How many times did we have to do stupid crap like this before we would be accepted? How many times before we felt like real basketball players? It was bad enough that as girls, we had to prove ourselves as athletes all the time. Now, even with a team of girls, we had to prove ourselves worthy by staying at some stupid school that had nothing to do with basketball. It all seemed so pointless, but she was right—it was one step closer. Jay and I were the same. We just wanted to play ball. I sighed. Tonight would be the night to make that happen.

I wasn't looking when Zach spun on his heels, and I ran into a warm, hard body. I bounced off his chest and looked up to see Zach standing in front of me with his arms crossed over his chest.

"What's your deal?" I asked, trying to step around him, but he blocked me.

"Hey there, Roadhouse." He flashed that lopsided grin at me and winked one blue eye shut. I didn't know how he did it without looking like a complete moron. He leaned down to whisper in my ear. "Can't wait to spend the evening with you." He pulled back and gave me a crooked smile.

"Get off her," Jay said, pushing him down the hallway as Bear grinned over his shoulder.

I rolled my eyes at Zach. "Come on," I said. He walked backward in front of me as I shooed him down the hallway with my free hand. He shoved his hand into his pockets. All he held was one paperback novel, and he let me walk next to him.

I looked up in time to see a group of junior girls eyeing Zach as we walked past them. They didn't even try to hide their stares. One whispered behind her hand as she looked at me.

"Do you guys think that place is haunted?" Bear asked.

"There's no such thing as ghosts, idiot," Jay said, shoving Bear's shoulder.

CHRISTINA HAGMANN

"Well, I, for one, am looking forward to an unsupervised night with the ladies." He waggled his eyebrows at Jay.

"You are such an idiot," she said, laughing. I knew Jay long enough to know what her flirting looked like, and it surprised me that she was flirting with Bear. He wasn't her type. She liked to be the center of attention, and he would be too much competition.

"Hey, Zach!" a sophomore girl who'd walked by us called out. "I love your jeans." I looked back at her, wondering when Zach had begun to draw so much attention.

Zach glanced at me before averting his eyes and picking up his pace to return to Bear's side. As I walked behind him, I studied his broad shoulders and the way his jeans hung off his hips. I quickly brought my eyes back up but couldn't help but wonder how I didn't see that Zach had become a full-grown man. Most of the guys in the ninth grade still had that lanky, scrawniness about them, but Zach had worked with a trainer over the summer, and I only just noticed it.

When we arrived at the locker bay, Zach and Bear moved to the right, but Jay gripped my arm, steering me to the left.

"What is it, you maniac?" I asked her, attempting to shake her vice-like grip from my bicep.

"Zach keeps staring at you. What's with that?" She scowled at me, studying my face.

"I have no clue what you're talking about." I looked away as we passed the senior locker section. Groups of students hung out between the lockers, and I even caught a quick make-out session between one of the other senior girl basketball players and her longtime boyfriend. I held my books closer to my chest.

"You want to know what I think?" Jay wouldn't drop it.

"No, but you're going to tell me." I finally made eye contact with her.

"I think that he's jealous that you're off the market. I think he's been waiting for you, and now he's afraid you're going to lose your virginity to Bender."

"Jay!" My mouth dropped as I slapped her on the arm, looking around to see if anyone had heard what she had just said. There was no way I was ready to do something I couldn't even talk about with my friend.

She shrugged. "Bender has a rep. I know you don't listen to what people say, but he does."

"I don't care about that," I said, but this wasn't the first time Jay brought the subject. Bender never once pressured me to do anything, but it was an added complication that clung to the back of my brain.

My thoughts returned to Zach as we were halfway to the freshmen row of lockers. I'd known Zach for too long. I'd known him longer than I knew Jay. Even though I couldn't think of him in that way, the note he wrote burned a hole in my pocket, and my mind raced with thoughts of what might happen tonight. What he might say in front of the others. Then I remembered my boyfriend. Bender would not be okay with me spending the night with Zach.

I sighed as I got to my row and rounded the corner. I waved over my shoulder at Jay, who continued to her locker one row down from me.

When I turned around, Bender was waiting at my locker.

Chapter 2

He stood tall, looming over the other freshmen, who were grabbing their things and eyeing him with suspicion. He wore a Henley shirt, and the form-fitting fabric emphasized his carefully crafted wrestling muscles. He smiled when he saw me. "Sam, I've been waiting for five like minutes."

I shoved him aside and opened my locker. "Sorry. My class is in the back hallway. I can't get here any faster."

"Dude, what's got you all pissy?" He tugged at my ponytail. "Hot date with your girl last night?" He leaned on the locker next to mine, and I could smell his cologne. It smelled like soap and man.

"Shut up, Bender. Jay's my best friend. You don't have to be a creep about it." Bender knew Jay had the hots for both guys and girls. Usually, he was pretty cool about it.

He laughed and flicked my cheek. "All right, all right."

"You could have given me a heads up. That's all." I threw my geometry book and my English binder in my backpack, still not looking at Bender.

"Heads up on what?" He grabbed the loop on the side of my jeans and tugged me around, so I was facing him. "What are you talking about?"

"You could have told me it's Freshmen Night." I held my backpack between us and pulled the zipper closed.

"How the hell am I supposed to know it's Freshmeat Night? That's a stupid basketball thing. I'm a wrestler." He pushed my backpack to the side.

"Come on." I finally made eye contact with him. "I know you guys all talk."

"Sam, believe me. I would have told you. You know I planned on you coming over tonight." He leaned down and kissed me on the nose, and my stomach fluttered. I tried to look away, hating public displays of affection. I knew my classmates were all trying not to watch. Bender grabbed my chin and pulled me closer. "You know what I planned on doing." His mouth stretched into a slow smile.

14

I looked around to see if anyone was listening and noticed Zach standing at the end of the locker bay, talking to one of his friends. He was watching us, and I wondered if his little conversation was a show so he could keep an eye on me.

"Hey," said Bender. When I returned his gaze, his eyes wandered to where I was staring, but Zach was wise enough to look away. "Would you want to go to the Tiki Hut for some food? I'm meeting some of the guys at five o'clock, so we'll have plenty of time. I'm buying."

I smiled at him, and he stuck out his bottom lip. When he looked at me that way, it was difficult to be angry. Bender had been my boyfriend since the middle of the summer when we met at the park, and I challenged him to a one-on-one game despite his height advantage. I beat him, and that's when I realized he wasn't a baller, but a wrestler. He did, however, have game. Too much game.

"Sure. I'll need it if I'm going to last through the night." I knew I was lucky as a freshman to have a boyfriend who could drive me anywhere. It gave me freedom, unless I wanted to do something without my boyfriend. I was used to Jay's mom driving us everywhere.

I slung my backpack over my shoulder, and Bender led the way through the locker bay. As he walked by Zach, he brushed his shoulder against him. Zach stumbled back a little but said nothing. He just stared at me as I passed him.

I gave him a little shrug as I walked by and then cursed myself for doing it. I shouldn't show sympathy. It would only encourage him.

Bender pushed through the doors and held them for me as we made our way to his hatchback sedan. I leaned against the car and watched him pull his keys from his pocket and open the door.

He turned to face me. "You okay?" he asked as he pulled the door open.

I nodded. "Yeah, I'm fine." The second bell rang, and I glanced over at the school building. "Can we get the food to go so I can go home for a while? It's going to be a long night. I can pay for my own," I added. I felt guilty. He was being so sweet, but it threw me off that he'd even noticed I wasn't happy.

He let go of the door, and it closed on its own. "Of course, we can get the food to go, but there's no way I'm letting you buy. It would ruin my rep." He pretended to straighten out his collar.

I rolled my eyes at him. "Like you have a rep."

He reached into his pocket and pulled out a wad of cash. "I have more money than you." He took my hand, turned it palm up, and what he dropped onto it shocked me.

"What's this?" I looked down at the money in my hand. There were over a hundred dollars.

"That's for you." He leaned down and kissed me. I couldn't think of anything to say, so I just looked up at him. Did he think I was that poor? My family didn't have a lot of money, but we were better off than a lot of families in Field Park. "What? You don't want it?" he asked, closing my hand around the money.

"No." I lifted my free hand to his face and pushed my fingers into his hair. "I just want you." When I said it, I felt self-conscious. It was super cheesy. Maybe I was overcompensating for the Zach thing.

He picked up the hand that was holding the money and kissed it. "I like you. You're a good girl, Sam. I'd do anything to make you happy."

My name always sounded so sweet when he said it, but I was a little annoyed with the implications. Did he think he needed to pay me off?

He pulled open the passenger side door and leaned on it, keeping it open for me. When I walked up, he ducked his head to kiss me. His lips were warm and inviting.

I smiled at him as he pulled away. "That was smooth." I tossed my backpack in the back seat of the sedan and climbed in.

He shrugged and pushed off the door, waiting until my feet were clear before closing it behind me.

He walked around to the driver's side, and I watched as he got in and buckled up. "I really do like you, Sam." He turned and winked at me before adjusting the rearview mirror.

"I like you, too." I wanted to tell him more than that, but I always made it a point to not give more away than necessary. But Bender was different.

He shook his head, and a slow smile spread across his face. "Nuh-uh. Don't do that. Just be honest, I can take it."

I smiled back at him. "I just said I liked you. Why would that require any more honesty?"

He turned the key, and the car rumbled to life. "You know what I mean."

I knew exactly what he meant, but I never gave in that easily. "Why don't you tell me?"

He threw the car into drive and pulled out of the lot. His answer was so quiet I almost missed it. "You are so beautiful."

I smiled. "Thanks, you are too." I meant it.

He glanced over at me and grinned wider. "Thanks."

I looked out the window and let myself enjoy his smile. He'd never say it, but I knew he wanted more than to have a good time with me. I wanted nothing serious, but Bender was hard to resist.

He reached over and let his hand rest on my thigh. I leaned my head back and turned it toward him. He looked over at me, smiled, and pulled his hand away. I was confused for a moment until I saw the lights flashing behind us.

"Really?" He reached into the glove box as he pulled to the side of the road right off the main highway. Grabbing his registration, he rolled down his window as he put his car in park.

I heard gravel crunching as I looked in the side mirror at the officer who approached the vehicle. I glanced at

Bender, wondering if he knew why we were pulled over. He hadn't been speeding.

The officer walked up to the driver's side door, and Bender smiled at me before turning back to him. "Hey, man."

"Bender." The officer nodded at him, then looked past him toward me. I smiled at him, and he nodded back before returning his gaze to Bender. "How you been?" he asked.

"Good. Just headed to the Tiki Hut for a shake." Bender turned his head and looked at me, then back at the officer. "This is Sam." He said it like he was introducing me to the cop, but I wasn't sure why the man needed to know my name. The two seemed to know each other already.

The officer nodded at me. "You know why I pulled you over?" He didn't seem as interested in looking at me as he was talking to Bender.

"I think I do." Bender leaned out the window a little, his arm resting on his door frame and his head turned so he could see the officer and still talk to me. "Sam was just telling me she hates cops."

My jaw dropped as I reached over and punched Bender in the arm.

The officer laughed and looked at me more closely. "Good thing you're not in Tyler County then, huh?" He winked. Tyler County was one county over, but I had no clue what he was talking about, so I just smiled and nodded, but said nothing else. The entire conversation was odd.

"So, what's the problem, then?" Bender drummed his fingers on his door, and I could tell he was getting impatient. I was too, seeing as I had limited time before I had to report to my night of hell.

The officer turned back to him. "There is no problem, man." He said it just like that, but continued to stare at Bender.

I saw Bender nod and shake his head. "So, can I go?" He was asking for my benefit more than his own.

"Sure." The officer patted the top of the vehicle. "Be safe, you two."

"Thanks, dude." Bender revved the engine before pulling away from the curb.

I rolled up my window and sighed when he reached over and took my hand. "What was that about?"

He shrugged. "That's just Johnny." He squeezed my hand. "He's a weird dude, but he means well."

21

I nodded and returned my gaze to the window, hoping he wouldn't notice my expression. There was something else going on, but I didn't want to press it. I'd heard stories about Johnny and Bender's father. There were rumors that Bender's father was dealing drugs, and Johnny was covering it up. Some rumors were that Bender's dad and Johnny had a relationship. The last time someone mentioned it to Bender, he punched out the guy's teeth.

I glanced back at Bender, and his eyebrows creased in thought. He remained quiet as he guided the car up the hill toward the Tiki Hut. It occurred to me that just like I kept secrets from Bender, there was a hidden side to him I wasn't aware of. The thought settled uneasily on my mind.

Chapter 3

The Tiki Hut was a small box of a building with some palm trees in the front and a grass hut roof. In the winter, they even put lights on the palm trees. Though it didn't look like much on the outside, there were a couple of pool tables in the back, and all the high school kids hung out there. The Tiki Hut was known for its shakes and cheese curds. There weren't many other options, but it was okay. The only other options for eating were supper clubs and bars. The former being too expensive to eat in, and the latter too smoky.

Bender pushed open the door of the Tiki Hut as dozens of eyes turned our way. The guys from the wrestling team huddled at the largest table. They yelled, "Bender!" as we walked across the room. Bender waved as we approached the kitchen. Some guys from the soccer team, sitting at the table in the corner, called out Bender's name. They assembled around a basket of greasy appetizers.

After sitting down, I leaned in, whispering in Bender's ear. "I'm still not sure about this." I wasn't shy, but sometimes Bender's popularity was overwhelming.

He looked at me and smiled like he knew what I was talking about. "It'll be fine," he said with a wink.

Everyone knew Bender. He had this chaotic charisma that people were attracted to. I wasn't even looking for a boyfriend when I met him, and that's what drew me to him. I planned on being single my freshman year and focusing on school and basketball, and then this guy approached me at the first football game of the season. I was walking to the concession stand on my own to get popcorn when this handsome boy-man approached me and asked me my name. I told him, and he introduced himself as Adam Bender.

"You play basketball, right?" he said, his cute smile making his eyes squint just a little. "And I assume you cheerlead."

Bender was a senior—I guess it wasn't surprising that he knew me. He was the star of the wrestling team, and I was on both the basketball and volleyball teams, though I had my picture in the paper from the time I was ten for national free-throw competitions.

"Yeah," I said with a slight blush. "I mean—no. I'm not a cheerleader." I stammered out my answer like some lame idiot instead of sounding confident and cool, like how he already did when he met me.

"That's cool. They're kinda annoying—all those poms and shit." He smiled some more, and I couldn't help but smile back. He had such a baby face that it made him look even younger than his seventeen years, but he had bigger shoulders than anyone I'd ever seen.

He asked me what I was doing after the game, and when I told him I was going to a friend's house, he asked if we could maybe hang out sometime next week. He handed me a pen, and I wrote my phone number on his hand as he watched me with a smile on his face.

I wasn't good at flirting, but Bender did enough for the both of us.

The next day, I walked to Lobel Park, down the street from my house, to shoot around. As I shot my fiftieth free-throw, I noticed someone on the jogging trail. Bender slowed to a walk and waved to me. I couldn't believe we were at the same place at the same time. It was like fate.

25

We played one-on-one, and that was it. We'd been to-gether ever since, much to the dismay of some of the upper-class girls, including Bender's ex, Natasha, and her best friend, Becca, who was captain of the basket-ball team. Hence my trepidation around public out-ings, especially so close to Freshmeat Night.

"I love this place," Bender said, walking back from the condiment bar, a stack of napkins in hand. His chair made a scraping noise against the tiled floor as he moved his chair closer and sat next to me.

As if on cue, a guy from the wrestling team strolled over, holding a pool stick in one hand. "Game?" he asked Bender. His name was John, and I knew him from my geometry class. He was one of the few seniors in the class.

"No thanks," Bender replied. "We're going to eat first, maybe later," he added as he nodded at me. John looked at us for a moment, then smirked -like some-thing was funny. He shuffled away and got another team member to start the game. I watched him and wondered what everyone thought about Bender and me. Jay's words came to mind, but then I pushed them away. Who cared what anyone else thought?

The server brought shakes to our table as we waited on the to-go order. Bender and I made small talk for a while, but he kept watching the door every time someone came in.

"You're not thinking about leaving me here alone, are you?" I asked playfully. He looked at me and grinned.

"I'm the one who talked you into coming tonight, right? You know I would never do that to you, baby." He leaned over and kissed me on the cheek.

I laughed and playfully slapped his arm. "Yeah, but now there are guys from the soccer team here too, so they'll probably try to hit on me if you leave my side for even a second." I was teasing, but I really didn't want him to leave me alone at the table. For the most part, I was comfortable in my own skin, but it was mostly upperclassmen in the Tiki Hut, and I felt like they were all staring at me in curiosity.

"You don't think they can handle themselves around women?" he said with a smirk.

"I'm just saying—don't be surprised if you come back to the table and I have a hickey somewhere on my neck, okay?" I was referring to one of the soccer guys who was notorious for marking his make-out buddies with deep purple bruises on their necks. Those poor girls had to coat the discolored markings with tons of makeup or risk a week's worth of ridicule. It was a wonder that anyone let the guy touch them.

"You don't think you mean enough to me that I wouldn't mark you as mine?" Bender said with a wink.

"You better not!" I said, feeling my face burn red as it always did when the jokes got too serious, but he just laughed and put his hand on my knee under the table and squeezed it before winking at me again.

Since I was incapable of flirting back—at least not without looking foolish or sounding conceited—we just kept teasing each other instead of trying to be sexy.

The bell above the door rang, and Zach walked in with a couple of friends. The glistening sweat advertised their trek from the school, and that and they were freshmen, so they couldn't drive. They took a table near us, and Zach stared at me as one of his friends walked to the counter to place an order.

A senior girl walked over by Zach's group and leaned on the table, sticking her butt out for the rest of the room to see. She was wearing a low-cut crop top that dared boys to look, but Zach looked oblivious as Bear leaned in closer to the girl. She kept patting Zach on the arm, but he held a forced smile on his face, glancing my way every few seconds.

While Bender babbled about something I didn't care about, I leaned my chin on one palm and glanced out the window at the cars angled parked outside on Main Street. I didn't mind that he loved to fill the quiet since it permitted me to listen rather than respond. I wasn't much of a talker, and Bender didn't need me to acknowledge him while he talked.

My thoughts turned to Freshmeat Night and the idea of staying in that old abandoned school all night. At least I'd have Jay with me. And Zach. When we were younger, Zach and I would spend all day throwing a football to each other. He was like my brother. And then, when we hit junior high, things changed. I started hanging out with Jay, and he hung with the other guys. When we were in the neighborhood, it was the same, but at school, it was like we were different people. Zach joined track and played football. He was a natural at every sport, but he excelled at basketball. It was strange that I was just noticing now that he'd turned into some kind of Guess model, and even though all the girls flirted with him, especially the upperclassmen, he didn't date. Why hadn't I noticed it before today?

I remembered when one of the baseball players and Zach's buddy, Tyrone Smith, asked me to go out with him. I agreed, anxious to get my first boyfriend out of the way, as many of my friends had. But Zach was strange about it, and when I asked him about Tyrone, he told me only the worst things about him, like how he had a stack of dirty magazines under his bed and spoke about going to third base with a girl at camp. And, while Tyrone seemed decent to me, Zach's remarks tainted my initial feelings, so I broke up with him.

I considered what Jay had said earlier. Could she have been right about Zach?

"Earth to Sam." I looked up as the server was lifting a basket of cheese curds off her tray. She put two glasses of soda down next to our shakes. I looked up at Bender and smiled like he hadn't just caught me daydreaming.

Bender's hand moved from my knee up to my inner thigh, and I lifted the menu up so it would block it. His hand slid under the table, and his fingers played with the bottom of my shorts for a few seconds before he grabbed his straw and took a drink from his shake.

The corner of my mouth turned up in a smile as I turned back to him. He leaned over and whispered in my ear, "I'm sorry—my hand just moved by itself."

I felt my cheeks heat up again. And, of course, he knew it. He was teasing me, but that didn't mean I liked it.

"It's probably because I'm wearing shorts, but if you play with my legs like that under the table again, you're going to get slapped," I said in a serious tone.

"What's up with you?" he asked me, dipping a cheese curd in ketchup.

"Nothing," I said. "Just thinking."

"About?" Bender shoved the cheese curd into his mouth and then sipped on his shake.

I shrugged and snatched a few of the cheese curds, dipping them into ketchup while I thought about how to answer him. I thought we were getting the food to go, but leave it to Bender to forget that important detail.

Bender looked like he was about to make some stupid comment but didn't when he must have noticed my serious expression. "Are you thinking about next year?" he asked me instead.

I froze as I popped the cheese curd in my mouth, then I nodded and took a sip of my soda.

"Don't worry about it, Sam. Things will work out. I'll be at the UW, and you can visit me."

"I know." I toyed with the wrapper of my straw. The problem was that next year I'd only be a sophomore, and I wouldn't even get my license until halfway through the school year. Plus, my mom would hardly let me go on a road trip right when I started driving.

Bender elbowed me gently, smiling. Although I knew better, I smiled back and nodded. Bender looked at some sophomore girls who were passing by on their way to another table across from us. When they had passed, he turned back to me and started discussing the Halloween party in a couple of weeks.

I looked around and caught Zach's eye again. His cheeks were red, and I wondered if he witnessed Bender's roaming hand. It was strange being here and not being able to acknowledge him as my friend. I looked away and took another sip of my shake. Maybe I shouldn't be so caught up in the future. I needed to learn to enjoy the moment. It was a tragic flaw of mine.

Chapter 4

After the Tiki Hut, we swung by my house so Bender could chat with my parents and sister while I packed my bag for the night. I had to give it to him. Most guys tried to avoid that sort of thing, but Bender genuinely enjoyed my family. I told my parents he was dropping me off at Jay's, and she told her parents she'd be staying at my house. They wouldn't check up on us. It was a Friday night, so my parents would walk down the street to the bar. They trusted me, as I'd never given them a reason not to.

I ran upstairs to my bedroom as Bender kept my family busy. I changed into comfortable jeans, my favorite Chicago Bulls Champion Sweatshirt, and my old pair of Air Jordans. They weren't really old, just from last season, so they'd become my street shoes.

I packed a change of socks, a fuzzy blanket, some cash, and a book. I had a bag of BBQ Corn Nuts on my nightstand, so I grabbed those, too. I closed my eyes, thinking about anything else I might need, and my brain flashed once again to the note Zach had given me and then what Jay had said. I tried to imagine me and Zach dating, but I couldn't picture us doing anything different from what we'd always done, going to Lobel Park to shoot hoops, watching the old Bulls games that my dad recorded on VHS, and going to the movies. Then I tried to imagine kissing Zach, but even my imagination was not that good.

I ran back down the steps, and Bender looked up from the photo album my sister, Dawn, was showing him. His grin was forced, and as I approached, I could see it was a picture of me, Dawn, Zach, and his sister, Susie, playing in a kiddie pool together.

"Dawn!" I yelled at her, leaning over and slamming the photo album shut. "Geez, we've only been here a couple of minutes."

"Sam, calm down," my mom said from the kitchen, not missing her chance to get in on the embarrassment.

"It's just a picture," Dawn said.

"No, it's not," I said. "I'm in my underwear!"

Bender chuckled, but I ignored him. Dawn rolled her eyes at me and handed the album to Bender. "Sorry," she said.

I glared at her as she got up and ran up the steps. Turning to Bender, I asked, "You ready?"

"As I'll ever be," he said, putting the album on the coffee table. I reached my hand out and helped pull him from the sunken couch cushions.

"Be safe!" my mom called as we walked around the coffee table to the front door. "And remember that Amanda is coming this weekend."

I'd completely forgotten. Amanda was my older sister who ran off after graduating and married her high school boyfriend. She was pregnant with their first child. She was one of the reasons I was careful about who I dated. I didn't want to marry my high school sweetheart. I wanted out of this place.

As we got in the car, I saw Dawn staring out the window at us. I shouldn't have yelled at her, but she could be so annoying sometimes without even realizing it. I'd make it up to her tomorrow.

Bender was determined to drop me off at the school, even though everyone else was being picked up by the upperclassmen. I knew it would be enough to piss some of them off, but Bender would take no for an answer.

As we pulled up to the looming vacant school, I fidgeted with my fingers. Shadows danced on the chipped old brick and what was left of the windows glinted in the receding sunlight. Fir trees stood sentinel all the way to the back fence that surrounded the school.

Becca stood in front of the group with her arms folded and a look of annoyance on her face. I let out the breath I was holding and said, "Bender, you didn't have to drop me off. They brought everyone else together." Plus, I was the last one, and I hated being late.

"Yeah, but I don't trust Becca, and you shouldn't either. She's always making shitty comments about you because I dated her best friend." That stung. I knew Becca was cold to me, but I didn't know she talked shit about me.

"All the more reason for me to go with them and not show up here with you. We don't need to remind her." I reached into the back seat, grabbing my bag.

Bender locked eyes with me, his tone serious for once. "You're too nice, Sam. You don't have to play into their shit."

"I don't. And you know I'm not that nice." I pinched him on the arm, and he pulled away from me.

"Damn it." He rubbed the spot where I pinched him.

He looked at the group standing in front of the abandoned school. "Wait, is that Zach Morris? You didn't tell me he was coming."

"Zach Markan?" I corrected him. A handful of seniors called Zach by the name of the star of the popular sitcom, *Saved by the Bell*. Bender liked to pretend he didn't watch the show, but calling him Zach Morris didn't help his lie. "Of course, he's here. He's only the best freshman basketball player in the state. He'll be leading the varsity this year. Why do you care? I didn't know you even knew Zach."

"What I hear is that Zach Attack has a little crush on you." He raised his eyebrow at me.

"Zach and I have been friends since elementary school. We've been playing basketball together since then. How do you think he got so good?" I mirrored him, raising my eyebrow at him. "Besides, you don't think I can take care of myself?"

"It's not that, it's just. Well, I don't like the idea of you locked in that school with those guys for the night."

"Honestly, Bender. I'd rather be locked in with some-one I know than someone I don't know. Like this Travis Stelly guy?" I nodded toward the guy standing by Jay. "What's he? A sophomore?"

"Smelly Stelly? Dude is harmless. He used to play football too at Littleford. Decent quarterback, but they don't have much of an athletic department. I hear that's why he transferred."

"I didn't know they made sophomores do this. Wait, is he actually smelly?" I wrinkled my nose.

"Just don't get too close, and you won't have to find out." He pinched the end of my nose, and I shook his hand off.

"Well, I better get going." He leaned over and kissed my cheek, but I pulled away as he turned to kiss my mouth. I knew everyone was watching.

He moved to grab the door, but I put my hand on his forearm, sitting on the armrest. "You don't need to open the door for me. I've got it from here."

"No, I'll walk you over." Staring at him, I motioned over my shoulder. Becca stood at the side of the group. Her hip jutted out, and she crossed her arms over her chest.

He grabbed my chin and pulled me to him, planting a juicy kiss across my mouth. I pulled away and smacked him. "That's not helping."

He smirked at me and watched me struggle with my seatbelt before unlatching it and jumping out of the vehicle. I raised my hand in a still wave, showing that everything was okay even as my guts gurgled in disagreement. Maybe cheese curds and shakes weren't the best ideas.

I made my way over to the edge of the group. They stared up at the old building looming on the hilltop. Becca said, "Have a good look, kids. Field Park Hilltop School was the high school until they built the new one over on the other side of town. The last students roamed these halls in the '70s. Rumor has it the reason the school shut down was because of the double suicide off the top." Becca squinted up at the top of the third floor of the building. "That's why the current school is all one floor."

We all stared at her. I'd lived in Field Park my entire life and had never heard of such a thing.

"I doubt that's accurate," Bear interrupted. "They would have had to build the new school before they closed this one. The double header didn't determine the one level." He grinned at Zach as Becca cleared her throat, and her lips pinched into a thin line. She was never the most pleasant-looking girl, but she looked overly annoyed tonight.

"Can it, Bear." She stared at him to see if he was going to interrupt her again, but he mimed zipping his lips instead. "You'll spend the entire night in here, and in the morning, I will come and unlock the door. Now, if there is an emergency, you can get out through the broken window on the second floor that leads to the fire escape. If you leave, there will be a punishment." Jay's eyebrows shot up. "And yes, it will be in the form of public humiliation, and the shame will travel with you throughout your high school career."

Becca paused again. When no one spoke, she strolled over to the trunk of her car and unlocked it. I watched, but I couldn't see what she was doing. Then she pulled out a bottle of vodka and five plastic cups. She walked over and handed us each a cup.

She started with Jay, filling each cup halfway.

Next, she filled up Bear's cup. "Wait, no mixer?" he asked.

"Shut up, Bear." She kept moving and poured the vodka into Travis Stelly's cup.

"Um, I don't drink." Bear nudged Travis, sloshing some of the drink in his cup. Becca stopped her pour and glared at him without saying a word. Travis opened his mouth, but then shut it again. When she was satisfied that he wouldn't utter another word, she finished her pour.

She moved to Zach, adding a little more to his cup. She eyed him as her tongue wet her bottom lip, and it occurred to me that Becca might have a little crush on Zach. Then she was standing in front of me. Being a forward on the team, she stood a few inches taller than me. She stepped closer, trying to intimidate me, but I didn't budge.

"You want some?" she asked. I could tell she wanted me to protest or to say something that she could hold against me, but I wouldn't give her the satisfaction. She began pouring anyway. When she was done, she stared at me as though waiting for something.

"Thank you, Becca." I nodded at her, and I heard Bear chuckling down the line.

She spun on her heel and faced the group. "Make it last, kids. It's going to be a long night." She clapped her hands together and smiled at us. "Now, follow me."

"Wait, where do we drain the snake in this place?" Bear asked as he took a step toward the school.

"There's a bathroom on the first floor. Obviously, there's no running water, but I'm sure it'll be fine."

Bear shrugged, but Jay looked at me and wrinkled her nose in disgust. We were used to peeing in the woods, but squatting in an abandoned building was different.

We walked in a line behind her as she led us to the chained front doors. She took her time, unlocking the padlock and pulling out the chain. Supposedly, the first seniors who came up with Freshmeat Night stole the key from the city center and had a copy made. Each year, they passed the key down to the next group of seniors so the grand tradition could continue.

Once we were inside, Becca held the handle of the door. "Any last requests?"

"Tell my mom that I love her," Bear said.

Zach smiled and stuck his lip out at him. "Dat's so sweet," he said, imitating a child.

Becca rolled her eyes and waggled her fingers at them before pushing the door shut. There was a rattle and banging on the door as she reapplied the chain. I imagined her clamping on the padlock with finality. That was something I wasn't expecting, being locked in. Zach turned and looked at me. He raised one eyebrow and smirked.

"Wait, they're locking us in?" Travis asked. "Is that safe?" He looked around at the rest of us, all strangers to him, and I felt bad for him. At least I had my best friend with me—and Zach.

"Eh," Bear said, slapping Travis on the back. "What could go wrong?" Travis stared at Bear as I turned and walked down the dark hallway. The rest of the group followed.

Chapter 5

"Sam, wait up," Bear called in the darkness. I stopped and turned around, facing the rest of the group. "We have to mark this momentous occasion." We waited for Bear to continue. "Well, cheers, everyone!" Bear yelled. He raised his cup in his hand, waiting for everyone else to raise theirs. We tapped the plastic together before taking a drink. I brought the liquid to my nose and inhaled. Big mistake. The liquid burned my nostrils.

"Blah!" Bear yelled, already having taken a big gulp. He shook his head, his cheeks and mouth making a flapping noise. "Yowza! That'll put hair on your chest!" He balled his hand into a fist and pounded his chest a few times. I took a sip.

Travis shook his head. "Yeah, I'm not drinking this shit." He turned to dump it out, but before he could, Bear leaned down and snatched it from Travis's outstretched hand.

"Alcohol abuse. Don't waste good hooch, man. We got a long night ahead of us." He took a swig from the cup and grimaced. "Well, what do you think? Should we all split up?" He grinned.

I shook my head. "You're an idiot, Bear." I glanced between Jay and Zach. "Hey, let's find the gym. I heard they have one working light in there. Some of the seniors got permission from the caretaker to use the court." Everyone nodded in agreement as we walked down the dark hallway. I didn't know if the permission thing was true, but it made me feel better about being here.

I took another sip, studying my surroundings. My sense of direction was not good, so I examined the walls, looking for markers so that I'd be able to find my way around the building. I walked out front with Jay at my side, and Bear and Zach were close behind us. Travis brought up the rear. There were a few stairs to the right that led down to what was probably the gym, but something caught my eye at the end of the hall. It was a flicker of white, and then it was gone. "Guys?" I whispered, looking behind me and then back down the hall, squinting my eyes in the darkness.

Jay and Bear both turned around, still holding their cups. "What?" Jay asked.

I pointed down the hall. "Just now... did you see something move?" There was nothing but silence for a moment, and then I heard the flapping again. "Did you hear that? It sounded like wings or sheets on a clothesline."

I turned and looked at Bear just as he took another drink. His cheeks puffed out, filling with liquid, and he smiled as he exhaled. I could see him cringe, but he finished the cup.

Zach moved in the direction that the sound came from. "Where are you going?" I asked, watching Zach walk toward the back hallway. He stopped at the end of the hall and kicked at something on the floor.

"It's just a pile of dirty rags," he said. He walked back to us. "That's probably what you heard. Maybe there was a breeze." He held up his hand to see if he could feel a draft.

I shrugged. "I guess that makes sense." I turned around to see Jay leaning against the wall, staring at me.

"You okay?" she asked. "You seem on edge."

I nodded a little too quickly, causing her to raise an eyebrow. "Yeah, I think the booze is just going to my head."

"You look a little flushed," she replied.

Bear moved closer to me, whispering in my ear. "It's just your imagination, Sam. Ghosts don't exist. Ghosts aren't—holy shit! What is that?" He looked over my shoulder, pointing. I spun and flinched, looking to where Bear's outstretched hand pointed, but the hallway was empty, and Bear doubled over in laughter.

Zach walked over to Bear and slapped him on the back. "Knock it off, man. We all gotta make it through this night together." He turned and shot me a sympathetic look, and I crossed my arms, holding my cup tightly in my left hand.

Bear turned and faced me. He must have seen how pissed I was because his mouth dropped in an O-shape. "Roadhouse!" he said. He opened his enormous arms and approached me. "I'm so sorry." He chuckled. "I didn't mean to scare you, honest. I was just joking."

As he got closer, I looked away from him, staring over my shoulder at the wall. That didn't deter him from wrapping his arms around me in a giant hug. My face pressed into his shoulder, and I felt him rub my back. "I'm sorry, Sam. Will you forgive me? Can we still be friends?" He rocked from side to side.

CHRISTINA HAGMANN

I pushed him away from me. "Get off me, you goon."
I couldn't help but crack a smile. Bear was just so dang
loveable.

He laughed loudly as he pulled away from me, his large
frame shaking with each chuckle. "I mean it, Sam. Jokes!"
He lifted both arms and pointed back to the small stairway
we passed. "To the gym!" he yelled.

Bear led the way, stumbling a little as he went. The
alcohol seemed to be getting to him, too. The rest of us
followed.

There was the smell of something burning in the air,
and I wondered if someone was having a bonfire nearby.
I felt a hand grab hold of mine, and I looked over to see Jay
holding my fingers. She gave me a small smile, and I was
thankful she was here with me.

Chapter 6

The light on the court worked and lit up the center of the court like a spotlight, but the shadows stretched around us, threatening to swallow us whole. We all sat in the circle at mid-court, nursing our warm cups of vodka. I didn't enjoy drinking, but maybe this would help me get through the night. I felt my tense shoulders relax as I clutched my cup and stared into the dark space beyond the court. The battered metal bleachers pushed up against the wall, twisted into terrifying silhouettes. I shivered.

"So, we're here," I said, trying to break the ice and get everyone talking about something other than how creeped out we all were. "Now what?" We all stared at each other. Everyone had a bag with them, and the bags scattered behind us on the court. I wondered if anyone brought anything useful or something to occupy the time.

"Truth or dare?" Jay asked, giving me a wicked grin. I rolled my eyes, but she pointed at Travis. "Travis. Truth or dare."

Travis looked around like he didn't trust any of us. "Truth," he said, but it came out like a question. Jay leaned forward, resting her elbows on her crossed legs. She studied Travis like an interrogator about to figure out if her suspect was guilty or not.

"Why did you move to Field Park?" It was an innocent enough question, and as truth or dare went, it didn't seem like a tough question to answer, yet Travis squirmed on his spot on the floor.

"I don't know," he said, not looking at anyone.

"What do you mean, you don't know?" Bear asked in a mocking tone.

"I mean, I don't know, okay? I moved here to be closer to my grandma. That's all any of you need to know." Travis looked down at his hands and picked at his fingernails.

"There's got to be more to it than that," Bear said, not taking Travis's hint, or maybe it was just Bear being Bear.

Travis looked around at all of us before leaning back on his hands, his lips a thin line. We all turned toward each other, trying to figure out what had just happened before all eyes turned toward me. "What?" I said defensively.

"Your turn, Sam. Truth or dare?" Jay asked.

"Dare," I said a little too quickly. I didn't want them asking questions about Bender. I knew where that would go, but I wondered if I made the right choice as my friends turned to each other and began discussing what they thought was a good dare for me—a dare they all would enjoy watching.

"Look!" Bear pointed to something in the corner of the gym. "A bottle!" He jumped up and ran across the warped floor, his shoes scuffing the floor with each lump.

"Why are you so excited about a bottle?" I asked, but as soon as my words left my mouth, I knew what he was thinking. "No." I shook my head as he ran back, holding a dingy old bottle that had probably been down here for years. "I thought we were playing truth or dare?"

"Come on. We're teenagers. That's what we're supposed to do." Bear pouted and placed the bottle in the middle of the circle. "I dare you to play truth or dare." I avoided Zach's gaze, waiting for Jay to speak up in protest. If anyone objected, it would be her.

Jay smiled at me and then eyed Bear. I looked at Travis, and he was watching Jay. I rolled my eyes and took another sip of poison. It burned going down my throat.

"Me first!" In his excitement, Bear forgot it was my dare. He grabbed the bottle by the middle and, with a flick of his wrist, set it in motion. The bottle stopped between Travis and Jay. "Tough choice, Smelly, but I choose the girl." Travis shook his head, not bothering to fight the nickname anymore.

"Thank the Lord," Travis said under his breath.

Bear crawled across the floor on his hands and knees, and Jay's eyes sparkled in delight. Last she told me, she had the hots for a girl on the volleyball team, but it was hard to keep up with Jay. She never knew if a girl reciprocated her feelings because Field Park, even in the nineties, was a pretty close-minded place. It was easier for her to tell if a guy liked her, and maybe she did like Bear. Even I had to admit he was funny.

She sat cross-legged and didn't move on his arrival. He got to his knees and inched closer to her. Now he was grinning as well. He leaned down and placed his hands gently on her neck.

"Wowza!" Zach yelled, doubling over in laughter. Both Jay and I began laughing, too, until Bear turned and shushed us.

"A little tact, if you will?" Bear said, addressing Zach.

"Sorry, sir." Zach saluted Bear and put his head down, but looked at him from under his tuft of hair that hung over his eyebrows.

Bear resumed his descent to Jay's face, and when their lips touched, Jay closed her eyes and leaned into his kiss. I looked away, thinking just how awkward this game was. The kiss lasted longer than it needed to.

When they were done, Jay grabbed the bottle and whirled it around. "Winner, winner, chicken dinner." It landed on Travis. There wasn't as much build-up as she leaned over and planted one on his lips. He looked disappointed, but it was clear who Jay had an eye for, at least this evening.

The wind was strong, and it pounded up against the windows that were still intact. Trees cracked in the gusts as the building clicked and clacked throughout. I was looking up at the ceiling, studying the rifts in the plaster, when Jay started calling my name.

"Oh, Sam. You've done it now! What will Bender think?" Her words were followed up with a cackle.

I glanced at the bottle that was now pointing in my direction and studied the four faces in front of me. When my eyes landed on Zach, he gave me a sheepish grin.

Of course. He couldn't have planned it any better. I was still feeling strange about the letter and what Jay had said about Zach. My thoughts turned to Bender. He trusted me. "I can't, you guys," I said, and I was telling the truth. Not just because I had a boyfriend, but because Zach was my friend. If I kissed him, that could change things. But also, if I ever kissed him, I would not do it with my best friend watching.

I looked around the gym for anything that could save me. A weathered basketball sat up on the stage that was under the hoop. I got up and jogged across the warped floor, trying not to trip on the lumps. I snatched up the basketball and took a few hard dribbles. It was flat, but it would work.

"Game of horse, anyone?" I asked.

Bear frowned at me. "You're no fun, Roadhouse," he said, pouting.

Jay stood and patted Bear on the shoulder. "Yeah, total vibe killer," she said, but she smiled at me.

Zach smiled and got up. He walked over and placed his cup against the wall, and spotted up for the shot. I tossed it to him with one hand, and he swished a three. He grabbed his rebound and waited for everyone to join him on the court.

"How about oldest to youngest?" Bear asked. "Smelly, that's you, right?"

"It's Travis to you, Bear. I don't do nicknames." He put his hand up for the ball, and Zach rocketed one to his outstretched arm.

"Okay." Bear shot the rest of us a look that said, *what's up with this guy?*

"I think I could take you, Bear." Jay puffed out her chest and gave her hips a little jiggle.

"That so?" Bear asked with a smirk.

Jay nodded and spotted up. Travis tossed her the ball as Zach shot me an *I sure hope she knows what she is doing* look. Jay caught it and shot a fade away. It fell through the rim as Bear turned and raised an eyebrow at her.

"My turn!" Bear put his hands up for the shot, and Zach retrieved the ball and passed it just in time for Bear to run in an arc in front of Jay, who had just turned around with a smile on her face. Her eyes sparkled, and I knew she was almost done with this game.

"You know you can't beat me, Bear," Jay said. "You've had more practice than me over the years, but it doesn't matter because I make everything! Boom goes the dynamite! That's what my daddy says about me, and daddy doesn't lie." She raised her arms in the air with a dramatic flair.

Bear studied her with quiet intensity and put up the shot. The sound of the ball clanking off the rim echoed through the gym as Bear looked on in disbelief.

Everyone broke into laughter except Bear. "Give me another. She was talking. That wasn't fair."

I took a few steps back as Bear begged for another shot. I thought I saw something move out of the corner of my eye and turned to search the shadows. There seemed to be something moving just beyond the light, shifting and swaying back and forth as if someone was watching us from the darkness.

I thought I heard footsteps on the stairs, and when I looked up at the mezzanine, a woman stood there, looking down at us. Her raven hair was in a loose bun, and she wore a simple white dress with a button-up collar. There was something strange about her face. It was fuzzy, almost like an oil painting.

I opened my mouth to speak, but no words came out. Someone stepped up next to me, and I looked over to see Travis staring up at the woman. When I looked back, she had vanished.

I looked back at Travis, and he stared at me, his eyes circles. "Did you see that?" His voice was soft, and I nodded in reply.

"See what?" Zach asked as he approached us. "It's your turn, Sam." He held the ball between his arm and his hip.

"There was a woman up there," I said, pointing at the spot where she'd just been.

"What are you talking about? I didn't see anything." Zach looked up at the mezzanine, then back at me. He bounced the ball to me, but it didn't have enough air to make it, and it rolled to my feet.

"No, I saw it too," Travis said. "A lady in a white dress."

"Don't be stupid. There's no one up there. Let's just keep playing." Zach was annoyed with us, like he thought we were messing with him. I bent over and picked up the ball, passing it back to him. Zach walked away, glancing over his shoulder at us before joining Bear and Jay.

I walked over next to Travis. "We didn't imagine that, did we?" I asked.

"No, I don't think we did. You didn't imagine those footsteps on the stairs either, right?" His voice was low as he stared back at me. "Someone is in here with us."

There was a creaking noise, and we all flinched before spinning to see a wooden door, painted the same yellow as the walls, slowly swing open. It had been concealed by the matching paint. Even the door handle was painted with the same yellow. The creak echoed through the gym like a wailing banshee.

"Did you guys notice that door before?" I asked. It stopped its arc, and we stared into the black void behind it.

"Yeah," Zach said. "But it wasn't open."

"What the hell?" Jay whispered. All of us stared at the door, not daring to move.

Chapter 7

We glanced at each other before creeping toward the open door. "Are you sure it wasn't open even just a crack?" I asked.

Zach shook his head, stepping away from us toward the door. Bear reached out and grabbed him by the shoulder. "Wait. What are you doing?" The wind whistled through the broken windows.

"I'm going to check it out," Zach said, rolling up the cuffs of the blue button-down shirt he wore over his Field Park t-shirt.

"Maybe we don't check out the creepy door?" Bear's voice ended in a question.

I stepped over to Zach's side. "No, he's right. If someone is messing with us, it's better we know now." I took a few steps toward the door, my adrenaline rushing through my body. I saw steps leading down, but they disappeared in the darkness. "It looks like it leads to a basement," I said.

"Basement?" Jay asked. "It's a school." She pulled her long hair into a ponytail that sat low on her neck. She looked ready for business. This was how she wore her hair in a basketball game.

"Schools have basements," Zach said, catching up to me. We walked over and stood in front of the door. "And boiler rooms." The rest of the group stood a few steps behind us.

Travis raised his hand. "Wait, why are we going to the basement?" He lifted an eyebrow, looking at us as if we were crazy.

"The basement is the scariest place and the most likely spot for ghosts or murderers. It's only logical that we check it first to make sure it's safe," Zach said before turning and smiling at Travis. "Come on. I'm just kidding. It's Becca and her minions trying to scare us out of here."

Travis eyed me. We'd both seen the woman, and it wasn't Becca, but maybe they'd recruited others to help.

Without waiting for an answer, Zach stepped forward into the doorway. "It's pretty dark down there."

Bear walked over to Zach and handed him his flashlight. "Your trusty sword, good sir."

"Why, thank you," Zach said, bowing. He pushed the button and pointed down the stairwell. "See. No ghosts down there."

We all moved to the doorway and stared down. After our eyes adjusted to the darkness, I saw cement steps just beyond our feet that led into the unknown.

"Is anyone else freaked out?" Jay asked as we watched Zach take the first few steps.

Bear stopped in front of me and reached back. "You can hold my hand, Jay." He waggled his eyebrows at her as she rolled her eyes in return.

I ignored him. "A little," I said. "I mean, I don't know how you guys feel, but the door freaked me out." I didn't mind telling everyone I was creeped out. These were my friends. Well, everyone but Travis.

Travis opened his mouth, but Zach's voice echoed into the room from downstairs. "Whoa, guys. Check this out. It's a room down here."

I pushed past Bear and walked the rest of the way down the stairs to Zach. "What is it?"

"Just a table, some chairs, and some lockers," he said, looking over his shoulder and smiling before turning back.

I looked around the room, seeing that it was a lot smaller than I'd expected from watching Zach disappear down the steps. Cobwebs hung from the ceiling, but Zach had pushed his way through most of them.

"What's that?" I asked, pointing to the hulking metal beast at the back of the dark room.

"That's the boiler. The firebox," Bear said. We all turned and looked at him, surprised by his knowledge of creepy school basements. "It's what heats the school and the water. Geez, it's almost like you guys forget my dad works for Field Park Heating and Cooling Systems."

Zach walked over to Bear and nudged him. "Not me, good buddy. I'm just surprised you learned anything from him." Bear grinned back.

"It's so dusty," Jay said as she walked into the middle of the room and stood next to me. She raised her hand to the wooden table and brushed off the dust.

"You guys didn't bring any chalk or something with you, did you?" Bear asked. "I mean, we could draw a pentagram on the floor if that's what they do in the movies."

Everyone looked at him. "Um, no?" I said, walking over to Jay.

"It's just a thought," he replied, shrugging his shoulders and walking back toward the door. "There's nothing down here, you guys. You know, I could go for some pizza right now," Bear said before pushing past us and making his way back up the stairs.

"Yeah, me too," Jay agreed, rubbing her stomach. Just thinking about food made my stomach gurgle. I watched the two of them run back up the steps.

Travis turned to me. "Are you coming?"

"I'm going to stay here," I said. "I just want to check out the rest of the room. Make sure there's nothing rigged."

"Why?" Travis asked with wide eyes.

"Curiosity killed the cat," Zach teased, poking his head between us.

"And satisfaction brought him back," I added with a smile. It was a saying we had when we were kids, usually followed by one of us getting in trouble for doing something stupid.

Travis shrugged and followed Bear and Jay out of the room and up the stairs.

I glanced back at Zach, who was looking around the room again. I walked over and began prying open the rusted-shut lockers. Zach did the same on the other side of the room.

The hinges were so rusted that they were crumbling with the first movement in decades. I jumped back as I pulled open a locker, and it fell forward, clattering to the lumpy cement floor and bringing up a cloud of dust. I waved the dust away, coughing up the particles that I'd inhaled.

Zach and I reunited at the center locker, the only one with a lock. It was an old combination lock, but it was rusted. I shook it, but it wouldn't budge. Zach reached around and picked up a metal pipe from the shelf next to the locker. He slammed the pipe on the lock. The noise shattered the silence of the small room, and I covered my ears with my hands.

The lock crumbled, and Bear called from the top of the steps. "Are you guys okay down there?"

Zach dropped the pipe and called up the steps. "Yep, just breaking shit."

"Cool," Bear yelled back. I imagined Bear, Jay, and Travis standing in awkward silence at the top of the steps, waiting for us to return.

I pulled open the locker and scanned the insides. There was a dusty old canvas jacket and a battered metal box crammed into the bottom of the locker. I reached down and pulled it out, but it slipped from my hand and clattered to the floor, opening and spilling the contents inside. Dust billowed from the box, and I backed away, waving my hand in front of my face to clear the swarm of debris that I almost breathed in. Zach caught me by the shoulders as I nearly backed into him.

I turned to face him, trying to speak, but dust caught in my throat. "Sorry," I croaked.

"I don't think that's what we're looking for," Zach said, brushing dust from my hair.

I coughed a few times before realizing that Zach was standing a foot from me, gazing down at me. I took a step back, bumping into the metal box.

I leaned down and picked up the box. There was still some residue inside, but there was something else. I reached in to dig it out, and I could see it was a tuft of hair. I dropped the box, scrunching my nose in disgust, and laughed nervously. "We should probably head back up so the others don't worry."

He nodded. "You're right. Unless you want to be stuck here with me?" I didn't answer him because he was giving me that look you give someone right before you lean in for a kiss. His stare was intense and made me want to squirm or look away completely, but I didn't. "So, this is a pretty crappy situation we find ourselves in, huh?" he asked.

"It's not so bad." I shrugged. "I mean—it could be worse."

"Oh, yeah?" He asked with a chuckle, running his hand through his hair. "How?"

I shrugged again. "We could be in this alone."

"Yeah," he said, nodding. "But then we couldn't completely rule out the possibility of us hooking up in here." He grinned at me.

I felt my cheeks turn red, and I turned my head toward the wall. This wasn't how Zach and I usually talked. We were honest with each other and real. This reminded me of Bender, and it made me uncomfortable.

He laughed, biting his lip. "This is going to be a long night," he repeated in a whisper, still looking at the wall.

"Yeah, it is." I nodded before glancing at my watch and then up the stairs. "Come on." I motioned for him to follow, but as I stepped on the first step, the overwhelming stench of something burning filled my nostrils. I coughed as though my lungs filled with smoke, though there was no smoke to be seen.

I looked back at Zach. "Do you smell that?" I asked.

Zach nearly bumped into me and looked up, surprised that I'd stopped. "Smell what?" he asked. He shook his head and took a step closer to me.

My nose wrinkled. "It smells like someone is burning food."

Zach's face scrunched up. "Um, no, it doesn't. I don't smell anything."

I shook my head and looked up the stairs. Bear's voice came from above, and he turned on a flashlight to peer down into the darkness.

"Hey, guys," Bear said. "What are you doing down there?"

Zach called up to him. "We're coming!" Zach put his hand on my shoulder, and I shook off the strange sensation that lingered with me. I breathed in, and the scent vanished, almost like it wasn't there.

When we got to the top of the steps, Bear asked, "Did you guys find anything down there?"

I looked at Zach before shaking my head. "No, nothing." He studied my face.

Bear narrowed his eyes at me. "Are you sure?"

"Yeah, I'm positive," I said, crossing my arms. I glanced at Zach out of the corner of my eye.

Chapter 8

Jay and Bear stood near us at the door while Travis stayed a few steps back. "Are you sure nothing happened down there?" Bear asked, raising an eyebrow at Zach while giving a nod.

I sighed in disgust. "No, nothing happened down there," I said, shoving him a few feet back.

"Ouch," Bear said, chuckling as he rubbed the spot on his stomach where I shoved him. "She's rough," he said to Zach. I raised my hand to hit him again, but a loud clanking sound came from outside the building. It sounded like someone was rattling the chains on the door.

"They came to check on us," Travis said, taking off toward the door, possibly hoping someone would let him out. We chased after him, but as we were about to turn the corner, Zach stopped me by grabbing my shoulder.

I spun around as he stared at me, his eyes wide open. "Do you hear that?" he asked, his voice low and serious.

"Hear what?" I asked. As he looked down the hall, he raised his hand to signal for us to be silent. My muscles tensed, and I stood frozen in place. The dragging sound was slow and deliberate, like something heavy being pulled across the floor. It was coming from somewhere inside the school, and it seemed to grow louder as it bounced off the walls of the hallway, echoing through-out the space.

The chains rattled again, and it jolted me from my spot as I took off toward the door. Zach's heavy footsteps fell behind me, and I ran the rest of the way. Travis was already there, pounding on the door. "I want out." Travis yanked at the door handle. "I always knew you Field Park kids were whack."

Bear caught up with us, and hearing Travis, he scowled at him. "That's no way to talk to your teammates."

Travis stopped long enough for silence to fill the air. There was no more clanking of chains or dragging noises.

"Someone is messing with us," Zach said, but he eyed me, as though willing me not to say anything about the strange sounds.

"Yeah," Travis said. "That's what makes it even worse. It's not enough to lock us in here for the night, but now they're going to screw with us all night?" Travis continued to pull at the door, even though it was useless. The chains were still there, imprisoning us.

Bear stepped up to Travis. "Hey, how do we know you're not part of this? Pretty suspicious that both you and Sam saw some stranger creeping in here. You coming from Littleford and all. Did you invite some of your old friends by for a visit?"

Taking a few steps back, Travis dropped his arm, his muscles still tense. Turning, he came face to face with Bear, who towered over him. There was a spark in the air, and Travis's fuse was exposed. "Are you accusing me of something?"

Bear stared at Travis but didn't answer. It was clear he wasn't going to back down, and he was a lot bigger than Travis. They were quiet for a tense few moments before Bear broke into a smile and slapped him on the shoulder. "I like you, Smelly."

Travis eyed Bear's hand. "The feeling isn't mutual," Travis said, but the corners of his mouth lifted slightly.

Zach clapped his hands together. "Okay, so if we think someone is in here, let's just do some exploring. You know. Search the place."

We stood in a circle. Jay was at my side, and Zach was on the other side. I listened in the dark for any more noises, but everything had quieted. If someone was messing with us, they were keeping a low profile.

"Hell no," Travis said, shaking his head. "I'm not going poking around this place. It's a freaking death trap." He was right. The sagging ceiling hung heavily over us, threatening to crumble at any moment.

Zach looked between Bear and Travis and turned to me as though I were the leader of the group. "It's not a bad idea." Bear shrugged. "Then we'll be sure no one is here."

I nodded. "Okay, that could work. Let's go back to the gym and make a plan."

"A plan? What are we, the Scooby Gang?" Bear laughed.

Zach shoved Bear. "Come on, man. You can be Scooby." Bear stuck his tongue out, panting, and we made our way back to the gym floor. I scanned the hallways and the balcony, but I didn't see anyone. I felt bad that we ignored Travis, but his hysterics could be contagious, and we had to remain rational.

When we got back to the gym, I looked around. "That's really weird," I said. My eyes scanned the floor. Everyone turned to face me.

"What?" Jay asked, moving to my side.

"The cups. They're gone." We looked around the gym. There was nothing, no bottle, no red plastic cups. Everything was gone. It made little sense. I turned and faced the others, who seemed as confused as I was. "They were here before."

Travis rubbed his head and grunted. "I told you someone was messing with us."

Zach shrugged. "I guess it means someone was here. But let's not get too spooked. I don't think it was a ghost who came to clean up our mess."

"Let's find them." Bear grinned. "Hide and seek!" he yelled out, and his voice echoed through the empty gym and down the dark hallways.

Travis's eyes grew wide. "Hide and seek? You've got to be kidding."

"What else are we going to do?" I asked him.

"I already told you guys, it's not safe here!" He turned on his heel and headed for the door, but Zach blocked the way.

"We're not leaving. We're going to find them, and I don't want you freaking out and making a scene." Zach straightened his shoulders, and I was surprised by how intimidating he looked. He gripped his flashlight in one hand, and the other hand hung empty at his side.

Travis glared at Zach. "I promise you won't have to worry about me freaking out." He started for the door again—this time, Bear stepped in front of him.

"Dude, I said I liked you, but this isn't cool. You're a part of the group now, whether or not you like it. We're all sticking together. Got it?" Bear loomed over Travis.

I held my breath, thinking Travis was going to punch Bear in the face. His fists clenched, and his knuckles were white, but Travis gave a stiff nod before turning and looking at the rest of us. "Okay, but we're not splitting up," he said.

Bear started, "But it would be quicker if—"

I cut him off. "We'll stick together," I said, nodding at Travis. This had to be hard for him, trusting a group of people he didn't even know.

Bear shrugged and turned away, heading for the stairs that led up to the mezzanine. "Let's just hurry and find who's here," he said.

We followed Bear, creeping up the stairs, trying to avoid the paint flakes so as not to make noise. Whoever was up there, we didn't want them to hear us coming.

Travis stopped in front of me. "Do you really think this is a good idea?" I studied him, trying to come up with the words that might calm him. "This is so ridiculous," he said to himself. "I can't believe we're doing this."

I put my hand on his forearm, stopping his muttering. "Yeah, but what else are we going to do? Sit and wait for them to scare us half to death?" I asked.

He looked at my hand. "I don't know. We should just leave. Didn't Becca say something about a fire escape?"

Everyone was still in sight, spread out along the hall. No one glanced back at our conversation. "Just keep going," I said. "That's all we can do right now." Travis nodded, and put I put my hand on his back, gently pushing him forward.

I trailed behind Travis as we made our way down the hall. His fear was contagious, and my nerves flared. The hall was so dark, but I could see the light of the flashlight in front of me and deep down, I knew there was nothing here but an abandoned school. Nothing scary about that. As I moved cautiously, I kept my eyes locked straight ahead.

I sidestepped a broken chair abandoned in the hallway, staring at it until there came a loud crash. I froze for a moment, trying to figure out what made the sound.

Zach pointed to his right, and in the classroom was an old coat rack. The wind must have blown it over.

Travis stared at me, and we both exhaled. There was nothing to be afraid of here. I kept telling myself that.

Chapter 9

Beyond the mezzanine were more classrooms lined with windows that looked out into the darkness. We had to rely on our flashlights to navigate the poorly lit back side of the school—the beams bouncing off walls with each step we took.

"We'll split up," Zach said, breaking the silence.

"I was kidding before," Bear said. "That is absolutely what we shouldn't do." Bear shined his light on Zach.

"We'll cover more ground. I'd rather just be done with this." Zach glanced my way before asking Bear, "Are you terrified, man?"

"I mean, yeah. I'm man enough to admit when I'm about to piss myself. No shame in my game." Bear's eyebrows shot up to his hairline, emphasizing dark-lined shadows on his face. Jay snorted a laugh, and Bear turned and shot her a look of surprise. "What?"

Jay moved closer to Zach. "Nothing. I just wasn't expecting you to say that. But, if it makes you feel better, I kind of think we should stick together too. The last thing we need is to run into each other and scare the shit out of ourselves."

Zach continued. "But if we're together, if someone is in here, they'll be able to hear us and move away. How about once we get to the end of this floor, you guys take the next floor, and Sam and I will do the third floor?"

I looked at him, considering his words. This was exactly what Bender wouldn't have wanted, me wandering around in the dark with Zach. It wasn't like they were shutting us in a dark closet together. We'd be moving from room to room, making sure no one was hiding in the building. But still.

Bear stared at the dark hallways in front of him, trying to imagine what would happen if one of them got lost or hurt or separated or worse. He shook his head and turned back to Zach. "Okay. We'll take Smelly with us too."

Travis shook his head and scowled. It was clear he didn't want any part of this, but he had no say.

Jay nodded, and both of them started walking slowly down one of the dark hallways. Bear kept his flashlight pointed at the ground in front of him as they moved cautiously, the silence only broken by their footsteps echoing in the hallway.

We followed, passing an open classroom on our left. Bear shone his light through it for a moment. Most of the furnishings were broken or missing, but there was still a desk at one end with a single book on it. Bear asked, "Hey, what is this room?" Jay moved ahead of him. "Does that say...'Dead Poets Society'? Not funny?" Bear asked. No one laughed at his attempt at a joke.

The next open door we passed on our left was a large room filled with broken furniture and shattered glass.

"Looks like the janitor wasn't too good at his job," Jay joked as we continued moving through the room, checking the dark corners for anyone hiding. Broken shards crunched under our feet as we walked, and Bear had to keep his eyes focused on the ground in case he tripped over any of the broken wood.

The floor plan was shaped like an L, and the hallway we were following turned sharply to the right at one end. Jay paused after we passed the room and pointed her flashlight at something on the ground. It was a stack of papers with handwriting scrawled on them. They fluttered in a draft. We continued walking until we got to the stairs.

Zach went first, testing their stability. They were cement, but there were cracks in them, and strips of paint and drywall from the ceiling were scattered about on the wide staircase. When we arrived at the next landing, Bear stepped aside and Jay followed. Travis looked between the groups and was begrudgingly moved by Jay.

"This is where we part ways. Wish me luck!" Bear called to Zach.

"You don't need luck," Jay said. "I have full confidence in you." Jay reached out and grabbed Bear's cheek, giving it a pinch before releasing him. He tilted his head and looked at her, rubbing the spot she'd just touched. Jay had already turned away from him. "Sam, can I talk to you in private for a minute?" The guys looked around, and I nodded, moving down the hallway, though it was impossible to be out of earshot.

She pulled me closer, keeping her head lowered and talking just loud enough for me to hear. "I just want you to take an honest moment to consider Zach. Bender is the king of the school, but Zach is the boy who would be king." She gripped my arm as she spoke.

I shook my head at her. "I'm not trying to think about that right now, Jay. You know that doesn't matter to me. Why are we talking about this right now?" I spoke through my teeth.

"It's just, I know when you met Bender, it was all exciting and new, but Zach is so much nicer than him. He'll be king of the school, and he'll actually deserve it because he will be devoted to his friends, namely, you. I just don't want you to wait too long." Though we were down the hall from the boys, and they continued their chatter, I noticed Zach eyeing me.

My brain briefly pieced together a fake history of Zach and me ending up together but stopped at where it would leave me if Zach and I broke up. I wrestled my arm away from her, leaving Jay standing alone, and walked back to where the rest of them stood, motioning to Zach to follow me up the steps.

"Goodbye, my love!" Bear called to Zach. Zach blew him a kiss, and Bear caught it, holding it against his chest.

I kept moving up the stairs with just my flashlight to guide me. We came to the third and final floor and made our way down the dark corridor. This level was weathered and worn. Mildew stains covered the walls and ceiling. I wondered if there was black mold. I heard black mold was deadly if it got in your lungs. I pulled my shirt up over my nose, shielding my lungs from the tainted air.

The first few rooms we passed were empty except for discarded chairs and papers scattered across the floor. Between most of the classrooms were small closets or what looked like offices. Those were even creepier than the empty classrooms. One closet contained a lone wooden desk, and strange symbols were drawn all over the walls. I imagined some bored teen scrawling the markings in the light of day in order to scare someone.

Zach paused in front of the window at the end of the hallway that faced into the main entrance of the school. This one was illuminated by the streetlights out front, and light flooded into the hall through the window.

"What is it?" I asked, joining him.

He looked at me and shrugged. "Just seems kind of silly to lock us in here like this if there's no reason to be scared. They've been doing this for years, right?"

"Of course." I tried to relax, but looking at the sidewalk below, chills broke out on my arms.

I must have looked terrified, because Zach chuckled as he moved past me toward another hallway that led to the opposite corner of the building. "Yeah, that's why we're going to be just fine." He waved his arm. "After you," he said.

By the light of the flashlight, we could only see sections of the hall, not the entire picture. Claustrophobia struck as something sharp connected with my shin, and I tumbled over, trying to catch myself. Zach was so close behind me he stumbled over me, and we both fell into a heap on the floor. Zach caught himself before face-planting on me, and as I lay flat on my back, I could see him hovering above me, the moonlight through the window washing over his face.

His hands rested on either side of me, and he stayed suspended above me, his eyes studying my face, searching for a reaction. My breath caught in my chest, and the fuzz in my brain prevented me from sliding out from under him. The world paused in this one perfect movie moment. Zach leaned closer. He lingered in case I protested, but I didn't. His full lips were soft on mine, and I may have even let out a groan. It fueled him as he parted my lips with his tongue and his body pressed against mine.

Zach and I made a great team. We worked well together. And now, we found another thing we were good at together. I felt the rhythm of our tongues, dancing and caressing each other. Electric pulses moved down my body. It wasn't this way with Bender.

I pulled away, suddenly remembering my boyfriend. Wiggling out from beneath Zach, he called my name with breathless words. "Sam. Sam, what is it?"

"I—I have a boyfriend." I sat up on my knees, facing Zach.

He sat up and ran his hands through his hair. "Bender's going to be gone next year. It will be us for the next four years. Why fight it? I know you felt that. We work so well together."

"We can't."

"I know how you really feel, Sam. Remember, you called me. Not the other way around. Just because we have conversations at night when no one else can hear them doesn't mean they never happened. I know why you picked Bender. I know you're afraid of falling in love in high school and never getting out of this town like your sister. Don't you see? That's the beauty in us. I don't plan on staying here, either. We both want out."

I stood, brushing off the knees of my jeans. "I can't lose you as a friend, Zach. I don't know if we could be boyfriend and girlfriend, but we can be friends. I don't want to risk that."

He stood up and moved toward me. We stood face to face as he spoke. "Since when do you, Sam Roadhouse Elliot, play things safe?" Zach grabbed my face with both hands and kissed me hard. The anger in his kiss faded as quickly as it had appeared.

I broke away again, panting. I pushed him back slightly, and he let me separate our bodies. "Since I found a good thing that makes sense." I was breathing as hard as he was. "I love Bender, and I have a good thing here, Zach."

He studied my face, and I could see surprise there. I didn't mean to use the word love. It was permanent. But if I took it back, Zach would get the wrong idea.

He rubbed his hands together, brushing the dirt away. "Okay, Sam. But remember what could have been. Never forget it because I won't let myself forget it." He looked hurt, and I regretted my words. "We better keep looking. Let get this done with." He turned around and walked away from me without looking back.

I brushed some of the dust from the knees of my jeans and followed him down the hallway at a much slower pace.

I was still a few feet down the hallway from Zach when a loud clanking noise, like someone slamming pots and pans together, filled the school. We both instinctually covered our ears. Zach turned around and looked at me. Then there was a shout, and it sounded like Bear's voice. We both turned and raced down the hallway back to the stairs, toward the sound of Bear's screams.

Chapter 10

We ran down the stairs, following the sounds of Bear's screams. Zach nearly landed on his face when he skipped the last four steps and jumped to the landing. I picked up my pace, wanting to help, but also out of fear of being left alone in the dark.

When we got to the landing, Zach pointed his flashlight down the hall, and we could see Bear standing right outside a classroom. Bear screamed again when he saw us approach from the hall, but he didn't move.

We jogged closer to him, slowing to be cautious. He looked okay, so I wasn't sure what he was screaming about. I glanced past Bear through the open doorway and saw it. Behind the door, a skeleton was hanging from the hook on the door. The head was on the floor, a few feet from the rest of the body.

It took me by surprise, and I yelped, jumping back and bumping into Zach, who stood behind me. He caught me by the elbow, steadying me before taking a few steps forward. I moved with him. When we crossed the threshold of the classroom, we could see Jay and Travis standing against the back wall in the classroom. Zach shined his flashlight back on the skeleton.

"It's a fake!" Zach shouted, finally finding his voice. He stepped forward and shined his flashlight on it, illuminating the metal pins that held it together. "It's just fake, you guys."

The room went quiet. "Of course, it's a fake," Bear said, shaking his head like he was trying to rid himself of the image of the thing hanging from the door. "It looks so real, though." He let out a nervous laugh as Travis and Jay stepped forward.

"Who would put a fake skeleton there?" Travis asked. "That's just creepy."

I was looking around the room, trying to find clues. I heard my friends speaking but only caught pieces of what they said. If someone put it here, they were long gone by now.

"I don't know," Jay answered. "Somebody who wanted us to believe it was real. Do you think we should take it down?" Jay asked.

"Well, if we leave it up, we might forget about it, and it'll scare us again. But then it's also here for the next group forced to stay here."

We looked around at each other, and in silent agreement, we all stepped forward to remove the skeleton. Travis and Bear grabbed at its legs.

"This is stupid," Travis said, his voice barely a whisper.

I leaned over, grasping at the discarded skull on the floor, when a cold mass of air hit my body as icy fingers tickled my spine. I stood up, turning the fake skull over in my hand, but when I looked down, I saw it wasn't just a skull anymore. Though the eye sockets were still empty, pale skin and dark hair appeared over the plastic. Even without the eyes, I recognized the face. It was the woman from earlier. The one only Travis and I had seen. I gasped and stepped back, dropping the skull back to the floor.

Everyone turned to look at me. Travis and Bear still held the skeleton in their hands.

"What's wrong?" Zach asked. I stared at the skull that was now just a skull. "It's a fake," Zach said with a laugh.

"You're scared of that?" I elbowed him in the side to shush him. I stared at the skull again, but once again, it was just a piece of plastic.

I shook my head. "Sorry. I'm fine," I said as they continued to lower the rest of the body to the floor. As I stared at the discarded objects, the rest of them moved about the room.

"Hey!" Bear yelled. "I think this was the teacher's lounge." He pointed, and I glanced up to see an old cigarette dispenser. "Dude, can you imagine? My dad was telling me how teachers used to smoke in the lounge. That's crazy." He pounded the machine with his fist, and it toppled over with a deafening thud.

I jumped, even though I knew it was coming. "Idiot!" I called to Bear, but he was already leaning over and picking something up off the ground.

"Hey," Bear called out. "Check this out." He held up a yellowed newspaper. Travis ignored him, but Zach and I were the first ones over to his side.

When I was close enough, I could read the headline on the paper. "Tragedy at Field Park School," I said, more to myself than to the others. I looked back at Travis, and he moved closer, and like the rest of us, he waited for Bear to say more, but he skimmed the page, reading to himself.

"Well?" I asked. "What does it say?"

"It says that teacher Mona Desden and her fiancé, Theo Lobel, fell from the top of the school. The police were still investigating and looking for more information." He passed the paper to me, and as I skimmed the article, he continued. "Yeah, they fell." Bear used air quotes to emphasize the word fell. "It's kind of creepy how they died together, but I guess they were in love. It's sad."

"Of course, it's sad," Jay said, slugging Bear in the shoulder before moving closer to me to get a look at the article. "That Theo guy is fine, though," she said.

"Hey," Bear said, rubbing his shoulder. "Is that Lobel, as in Lobel Park?"

"Dude must have had bank," Jay said.

Using my flashlight, I studied the photos for a moment before moving the paper closer to my face and squinting at the photo. It was her. Mona Desden. She was the woman I saw in the mezzanine. It was her face in the skeleton.

Something strange was going on, but I was no longer convinced it was a figment of my imagination.

Chapter 11

The sound of heavy breathing filled my ears, and it took a moment to realize it was my own. Closing my mouth, I turned the photo to Travis, straightening the paper so he could clearly see. "Do you recognize her?"

He glared at it for a moment before shifting his gaze back to me. With a nod, he took the article from my hand and began reading it. I pointed my flashlight over his shoulder.

Zack stared at Travis and me, trying to decipher our unspoken language. His hand reached out, and he pulled the corner of the paper closer so he could see it. "Who is she?" Zach asked.

Travis bit his lip before whispering. "The woman we saw earlier. That was her."

Something had clearly shaken Travis. His hands were shaking and his voice was unsteady as the weathered edges of the old paper crinkled and ripped under his tight grip.

Bear brushed some dust off the table, pushing a cloud at Travis. "That's impossible. She's dead." He snorted at his own words, but no one else joined him.

It was quiet in the room as Travis stared at the woman in the photo. The image captivated him, his gaze never leaving her face. I glanced around. I thought I saw a figure standing near us out of the corner of my eye. As I turned around, I saw only what I had seen before—an empty chair next to Bear and a table full of scattered papers. It must have been a trick of the light. Maybe a shadow formed by the motion of our flashlights.

Travis remained mute with his eyes glued to the picture.

"What's up?" Bear asked, interrupting the silence. "What's wrong, Smelly?" He moved closer and grabbed Travis by the shoulder.

"She's the woman we saw, Bear. I swear." He handed the paper to Bear so that he could inspect the photo.

Bear looked between Travis and the paper. Cold air whistled through the shattered windows, and the streetlight outside flickered, producing a moment of darkness that broke Bear's trance. "Bullshit." He snagged the paper and crumpled it up, and without hesitation, he shot it into the trash can next to him.

"What are you doing?" Travis asked. He stepped toward Bear, going nose to nose with him, or nose to neck, because of the height difference.

Bear said, "There are no ghosts. There are no skeletons. It's just an old rundown school and we're going to go back to the gym and wait the rest of the night out there." Bear crossed his arms, nudging Travis.

Zach stepped in between the guys, creating space for himself. "Guys, chill," Zach said. "There's got to be an explanation. Maybe there's a projector set up somewhere. I heard that people have done that to simulate ghosts. Let's go look and see if we can find anything." He turned to Bear. "Dude, apologize to Travis."

Bear stared at Zach. "Why? The boy is getting on my nerves."

"Boy?" Travis said. "I'm older than you." The wind picked up outside, making a howling noise against the broken fragments of the building.

"Whatever." Bear shrugged. "Just stop saying there are ghosts before I knock all of your teeth out."

"Bear, knock it off." Zach pushed Bear in front of him, leading him out of the room.

"That kid is annoying. I tried to be nice," Bear said, as though Travis couldn't hear him. "He's as dumb as a box of rocks."

"Bear," Zach said quietly, but even though Bear was calming down, there was no stopping his comments.

"And he's being a wimp. I think they planted him in here to scare us," Bear said. This time Zach said nothing, and I thought about his words. Travis seemed nice enough, but he was the only one present I didn't know. Deep down, I hoped Bear's words were true, because it would be less frightening to know that Travis was the one doing all this rather than actual ghosts.

Jay linked arms with Travis, leading him down the hall. "Ignore him," she said. "That's just Bear being Bear. He's only acting that way because he's scared."

"I heard that!" Bear said, turning around, but Zach grabbed him by the shoulder of his windbreaker and pulled him down the hallway.

Jay steered Travis down the hallway. "Becca said something about the fire escape. It should be right over this way." While stepping around debris in the hallway, she pointed. She pointed to a door at the end of the hall-way. There was a partially torn sticker on the door that read "Fire Escape."

Travis let go of Jay's arm and ran to it, pushing his body against it. When it didn't budge, he jiggled the handle.

"What's wrong?" Jay asked.

Travis bent over and slammed his shoulder into the door, grunting with the effort. "It's stuck," he said, between breaths. He turned and faced us. "There's no way out."

Despite his best efforts to appear calm, the panic was clear in the lines of his face.

Jay stepped toward him again, and I joined him on the other side. Zach even stepped closer before saying. "Hey, we weren't going to leave anyway, right? But there's probably some broken windows on the first floor." Travis stared at him as though trying to process his words.

He slammed into the door once more, and it banged open. Travis pitched forward, and I caught him just as he was about to plummet into the open air. There were no steps. Travis reached back, grabbing for the doorway and pulling himself back. I glanced over the threshold of the door to see the metal stairs in a heap on the ground far below.

Travis backed away from the door, wheezing. "Thanks," he said to me.

"I guess no one has checked on the fire escape in a while." I laughed nervously, even though Travis could have been seriously injured in the fall.

"Come on," Jay said, addressing us. "Let's head back to the gym."

Travis's expression was unreadable as he trailed behind us. I walked behind the group, aware that something might sneak up behind me. However, when I spun around, there was only moonlight and a glow from the streetlights streaming into the hall from the classroom's windows.

Chapter 12

When we arrived back at the gym, we spread out, determined to wait out the rest of the night in the spotlight of general safety. Jay and I sat apart from the boys. Bear and Zach sat at center court, and Travis stood closer to the wall, examining the strips of paint hanging from the wall like streamers from a bygone party. I struggled to imagine the gym in its glory days. Fans packed the stands to watch some small-town hero hit the big shot. Someday, I'd be that player.

Growing up, I understood my parents didn't have the money to send me to school, so it was up to me. Although I did well academically, I was sure I was not doing enough. That's when I discovered basketball. It had been my dream ever since. That was why I was in this gym tonight with a bunch of other dreamers. It was why, like the rest of them, I couldn't just leave. This night defined my freshmen year.

Jay flicked my kneecap, and I looked over at her. "What?" I asked.

She nodded toward Travis, and I watched at him again before turning back to her. "What?" I asked.

"I know what he's hiding," she said. "Don't worry. He's not a serial killer."

"I didn't think he was," I said, waiting for her to share the secret.

"Hey, what I said about you and Zach before? I meant it." She rested her elbows on her crossed legs as I hugged my legs closer.

"You can drop it. I'm not interested in talking about it." My face grew warm, and I was sure my ears turned red.

"I know you're not thinking this through, that's all," she said. I sighed, glaring at the wall and knowing I couldn't stop Jay from what she was about to tell me. "I know you don't want to risk your friendship. I get that. But what you don't understand is that as soon as some girl latches on to him, you'll lose a piece of him, anyway. Just like he's already lost a piece of you. Why do you think he's trying so hard? He thinks this is his last shot."

I turned to face Jay, surprised that she had such a clear perspective on my relationship with Zach. Usually, I tried to be so rational, but Jay was able to embrace her feelings and thus understand others better than me.

"Why can't we go back to the days when we just talked about basketball?" I asked.

"Because we're growing up. And because guys are obsessed with you." She delivered the last line with a straight face, but when I leaned over to slap her, a smile broke out on her face.

"You should talk," I said.

"Yeah, but I'm not like you. I'm not on the market for a relationship."

I was about to change the subject and ask her what Travis's secret was when Travis cleared his throat, interrupting my thoughts.

"I think I might leave," he said. All eyes turned to him.

Zach spoke first. "You don't have to leave, man. We're in this together. Let's take shifts and get some sleep."

Bear barked out a loud laugh that echoed in the gym. "Yeah, right! Sleep." Zach shot him a dirty look.

"I don't know, you guys." Travis was shaking. "Something bad is gonna happen. Can't you can feel it?"

"Travis," Zach said, looking at him. Travis looked up at him. "You're with us, right?"

Travis shook his head. "I can't." He dropped his head and studied his fingernails. The rest of us looked at each other again, but before anyone spoke another word, the walls lit up with a flash of headlights. We all looked up at the broken windows and the red and blue lights that flooded the gym.

"Come on!" Zach said as he ran across the gym to a small doorway under the hoop. He flicked the light off, plunging us into darkness save the streetlights outside that shone like beacons through the windows. I glanced at the wall above the door and noticed a small rectangle window. It looked like an old projector room. Zach opened the door and waved us up.

Travis was in the lead but halted on the threshold, shaking his head. "I'm not going up there."

"Dude," Bear said, "if the cops catch us in here, we could all get fined. Plus, we've been drinking. Do you want to have to sit out your first three games?" Bear pushed by Travis, not waiting for an answer, and took the small steps two at a time. Jay followed without hesitation.

I grabbed Travis by the arm and pulled him with me, expecting him to resist, but he followed, and Zach took up the rear, closing the door behind us. The darkness swallowed us.

When I entered the small room, a rectangle of light on the floor from the gym was a dim glow in the room. I let go of Travis, knowing that he wouldn't run now that he was crammed in here between us. Bear stood by the window, trying to look out it. He was the only one tall enough to reach it without a step stool.

The musty smell of the old projection room offended my nose as we huddled in complete darkness, terrified, awaiting the creak of the steps signaling the approach of something sinister. Zach's heavy breath warmed my neck as his hand found mine. I squeezed in return.

A car door slammed, followed by the creak of the front doors. Bear turned and glanced our way. The confusion on his face matched mine. How could anyone get in with the chains on the door?

It occurred to me that Becca, or one of the other seniors, might come to check on us, but Bear's words cloyed on my brain. I couldn't get caught in here, and I couldn't afford to get busted for drinking. I'd been so stupid. No wonder they gave us alcohol when we first arrived.

There was a tap of shoes across the broken tiled floor at the front of the school. Whoever it was, they weren't approaching the gym floor but walking across the mezzanine.

"What are you doing here?" A woman's voice echoed up to our hiding spot. I held my breath, straining to figure out if the voice was familiar.

A man's voice answered. "I came to see you. Why? Are you surprised?" The muffled conversation drifted away.

Our heavy breathing filled the small space. For minutes, no one spoke. I asked, "Should we go check it out?"

"I think that would be a bad idea," Zach whispered back. "We have no clue who those people are. Let's just wait here until they leave. It shouldn't be too much longer."

Jay whispered back. "We don't even know who that was. What if we get in trouble for being in here?"

Finally, Travis spoke again. "Who cares? At least we'll get out. And we can't be called chicken if they make us leave. Plus, I wasn't even drinking." Travis's logic was sound, but it wasn't that simple. Becca would probably blame me. Cops could be involved.

"Well, I'm not staying up here all night," I answered as I let go of Zach's hand. "I'm going to check it out. I'll give you guys the all-clear."

"I'm going with you." Zach's voice came from closer than I expected, and a tingle shot down my spine.

I led the way down the chipped steps and back to the gym floor, glancing toward the mezzanine before moving to the stairs. We walked all the way around to the front and peered down into the long hallway, hearing nothing but our own breathing.

A slamming door on the level above us made me jump, and I reached for Zach, but he was just beyond my fingertips. He looked down at my hand, and I pulled it back, embarrassed.

"Maybe this was a bad idea. Should we go back to the projection room and wait a little while?" I asked.

"Let's just check out upstairs. We can be quiet. If we see anyone, we run." His voice was shaky but determined.

I nodded in return and led us through another door and began climbing the back stairs, using whatever light made its way up through ancient windows as a guide. This stairwell was narrow, and I wasn't sure where it would come out. The school had grown maze-like in the dark.

When we arrived at the top step, the door was slightly open. I reached for the flashlight in my back pocket, but Zach caught my hand. "Don't," he whispered. "Someone might see." He pointed toward the windows.

"You don't know that they will. Besides, they might have left already," I said.

Zach hesitated for a moment before he responded. "But they might not have. Let's be quick and no flashlights."

I glanced at the light in my hand and nodded in agreement. We slipped in through the open door and began searching for any clues to whose voices we heard.

Every shadow looked like a person crouched in wait, but the voices remained silent. Each crunch of my shoe on shattered glass from the old windows could alert anyone to our presence. Zach waved me forward, and I didn't know how he could see anything in the dark.

I heard a muffled yell and moved faster. I had the sudden feeling that whoever the voices belonged to, they were no danger to us. The classrooms looked empty, but it was difficult to tell with the shadows in the corners. I mouthed my words silently. "Do you think that's where they went?" I asked, pointing to a nearby room.

Zach's eyebrows sat low on his forehead as he leaned close to my ear and whispered. "There's something strange going on here."

We moved through the shadows to an empty classroom, and the voices grew clearer the closer we got to the windows. The man's voice was obviously angry as he yelled about someone named Casey, but I couldn't hear what he said next because of Zach's hand pressing against my mouth from behind me.

"What are you doing?" I whispered into his hand, but he didn't answer me.

The woman's voice was much higher and turned pleading. "I told you there's nothing going on." Her words were cut off as though someone had stopped her from speaking.

Zach clasped his hand against my mouth as I struggled to lean away from him, but his grasp just tightened more around my waist until the struggle wasn't worth it anymore.

"You're such an idiot," the man said with venom in his tone. "We would have been happy."

My heart beat faster, but Zach began pulling me backward toward the door. I pried at his hand, trying to remove it from my mouth. I needed to know what was going on.

As if he knew what I was thinking, he put more pressure on my neck as he tugged me along with him as quietly as possible, retreating back down the hallway.

When we neared the stairwell, he released me, and I turned around to face him. "We have to help her."

Zach hesitated as he looked back over his shoulder in the direction we had come from. "No." He took me by the hand and pulled me down the hallway as I glanced over my shoulder.

Chapter 13

H e pulled me back down to the gym, where the rest of the group waited for us on the gym floor. They no longer hid in the projection room. When we got there, I shook Zach's hand from my own and spun on him. "Why didn't you let me go after them?"

Zach stared at me. "Are you kidding, Sam? I'm protecting you." He stepped closer, but I backed away.

"I don't need you to protect me," I said. "I need to know what's going on, and I need to know who's sneaking around this building." Everyone was staring at me, but for once, I didn't care.

"What happened?" Jay asked, stepping closer to me and blocking me from Zach. She was in protective mode, and I was grateful for that.

"There were voices. A fight. I think it was Mona," I said, glancing at Travis to see if he reacted.

The room was still, and even Jay studied me like she wasn't sure if I was joking or not.

Travis's eyes grew wide. "No, man." He shook his head. I stepped to him, reaching out, but he pulled away from me. "I'm out of here. I'm out. Done. I don't care." Turning away from us, his tennis shoes echoed rhythmically as he stomped away from us toward the doors. I had no clue what he was going to do when he got there. The doors were still chained and the fire escape had proven to be unsuccessful, so there was no way out, but he kept threatening to leave. I wasn't sure what his plan was.

"Let him go," I said. He'd reached his limit, and though he was complaining all night, his tone was different this time. We watched him go, and when he rounded the corner and was out of our sight, Jay looked at me with questions in her eyes, almost like she expected me to chase after him.

We listened for his footsteps, but he must have gotten to the door because the school was quiet except for the creaks and groans of the old structure fighting to stand in the night breeze. The high ceiling loomed above me, and

I couldn't help but feel unease. There was a reason they boarded it up, and I wondered if anyone had considered that one day it might just cave in on an unsuspecting group of teens forced to spend the night inside.

From out in the hallway came a soft grunt and the thud of something hitting the floor. I held my breath, thinking that maybe Travis had plopped down by the door to camp out. I looked at Zach, and his mouth dropped open as though he was going to speak.

"What was—" I started.

"I don't know," Zach said quietly, not waiting for me to finish my question.

"Did you hear that?" I whispered to Jay, just to make sure my mind wasn't playing tricks on me.

Jay looked around the room, her eyes finally stopping at mine. "I think we should go after him. What if he fell or something?"

"Travis!" I called. We ran in the direction that Travis had gone. When we arrived at the corner, I saw part of the hall in front of us, including the doors. There was no one there. An odor hit me in the hallway. It smelled like burned hair or smoky dirt. "Hey!" I called again and then felt Zach grab my hand.

"Where'd he go?" Bear asked. Even though Travis had annoyed him, Bear was worried. "I don't see him. There's no way he just disappeared."

We looked around, and Zach stepped forward and pulled the handles, the chains catching on the outside. "Well, he didn't go through the door." Zach didn't look concerned, and it struck me as odd.

I stepped closer to Zach. "What's up with you? Why aren't you more worried about him?" I asked him.

Zach stared at me for a minute before running his hand through his hair and letting out a sigh. "I am worried, but I don't want to be tricked. He still could be a part of all this."

"What?" I asked. I thought we were past all of this speculation. I thought he realized that what we heard and saw was not a bunch of teens playing tricks on us.

"Sam, the figure on the mezzanine. Did he see the figure first?" Zach studied my face.

"If you're suggesting that he saw it and I agreed with him, I know myself a little better. I'm not that impressionable." It offended me that Zach even implied that Travis could have tricked me.

"Sam, look at me. I know you aren't some ditsy girl who would agree with whatever a guy says." Zach stared right into my eyes as he said spoke, and his voice had a low tone to it. "I'm just saying that if he's part of this, there could have been some projector and because he was guiding you, maybe you believed it a little more than you should have."

"No, that's bull, Zach, and you know it." I pushed by him.

Zach grabbed my arm. "Sam!" he said, and it sounded like he meant for me to stop, but when I looked at him, his eyes were focused on something over my shoulder.

I turned around and saw Jay walking back toward us. She stopped in front of us and tilted her head to the side like she was waiting for something.

"What's wrong?" he asked.

"Instead of standing there arguing about your bullshit theories, we should comb this school for him." Jay stepped closer to me.

"We already searched the school," Zach said.

I looked at Jay, nearly forgetting that my best friend was at my side because Zach was consuming my thoughts. I pushed him out. "Let's go then. Let's find Travis." I turned back to Zach. "Let's go, Zach. We can talk later. We should find him and focus on that instead of arguing about how we may or may not be in danger here."

Zach looked at me and then followed Jay as she headed out of the school entryway. I walked after them, feeling my heart race with every step. He wasn't by the front doors, so we moved to the stairs and paused, peering up at the darkness on the second floor, wondering what we would find.

"I'm going up," Jay said and then climbed the stairs, one at a time. She stopped when she reached the top and waited for us to reach her before heading down the hallway.

We were on the mezzanine, looking down at the gym, when the sound of movement below caused the four of us to stop.

Someone stood at the entrance of the gym where we stood only minutes ago. We all watched as a shadow walked across the gym floor. "It's him," Bear whispered. "How the heck did he sneak by us?"

"Travis!" Zach called, but Travis didn't look up. He continued walking to the corner of the gymnasium, toward the basement door.

I could tell that Jay was about to say something in response, but before she got the chance, a noise came from under the building. It sounded like metal being dragged across concrete, and I looked at the others before turning back toward Travis. There was nothing there.

"Did you hear that?" Bear asked.

"Where did he go?" I asked, feeling the fear building in my chest.

"Come on," Zach said, slapping Bear's shoulder as though this was all a game. "He went into the basement."

"But he didn't even have a flashlight. Why would he do that?" Jay asked.

Zach shrugged before jogging back down the steps to the gym. We all followed, and when we got there, the moonlight was shining in through the windows on this side of the building. I could see better. The bleachers were torn up near one wall, and there were random pieces of wood strewn about on the floor. It seemed as though the gym looked different every time we returned to it, but it had to be my imagination.

Zach spoke first. "Bear and I will go check out the basement. You two stay here." I opened my mouth to argue, and Zach gave me a pleading look. I nodded, and the two boys took off toward the basement door.

"What the hell is going on?" Jay asked. "Everyone is acting crazy. Even you're being weird."

I rubbed my arms, chilled in the cavernous gym. "I swear to you. The voices we heard. They aren't real people."

"So, you're saying there are ghosts? And you went chasing them? Why, Sam? Why don't we get the heck out of here?" She grabbed at her ponytail and smoothed it out.

"I don't think we can," I said, looking around at the shadowy corners that crept closer to us. We waited in silence—my final words echoing in my brain.

The boys returned in under ten minutes. "Well?" I asked.

"There's nothing down there," Bear said.

"That's impossible. There was nowhere else for him to go." I looked at each of them before my eyes settled on Zach, his face looking like he was about to say, I told you so.

"He's messing with us," Bear said. "He's got to be."

Jay looked at me, shrugging.

I said, "Okay, so where did he go?" I crossed my arms and looked at Zach. "If he's messing with us, where did he go? How can you explain this?"

"There's got to be projectors. We haven't even explored this whole place. Who knows? There might be a room where a bunch of people are hiding and plotting." He looked up and spun around. "They could have cameras on us right now!"

A loud crash came from above us, punctuating his words.

"See?" he said as he narrowed his eyes at Bear.

"Let's go find these assholes," Bear said, slamming his fist into his palm. Before we all agreed, Bear and Zach took off running back up the steps. Jay looked at me and raised her eyebrows.

"Let's go," I said, throwing up my arms. Jay followed me without hesitation.

Chapter 14

When we caught up to Zach and Bear, they stood outside the first doorway.

"I think the sound came from in here," Zach said, shifting his weight from foot to foot.

"Totally," agreed Bear. He held his flashlight under his face to create a spooky effect as we approached them. The beam from his flashlight danced across the warped and dirty glass windows that lined the outer wall. Zach slugged him in the arm. "Ow," Bear said.

Zach moved first through the doorway, with the rest of us following behind him. The dark room smelled like mold and unswept floors. "What is this place?" Bear asked.

I walked over to the dust-covered desk in the back of the room. One leg was broken off, and it sat at a slant. "Maybe there's something left behind in a drawer." I opened the first drawer, and Bear pointed his flashlight, so I could see what was inside. There was a pin with a name on it. It read, Ms. Desden.

I looked up at Jay and Bear before my eyes settled on Zach. "This is her room. The woman in white. Mona Desden."

Jay's eyes widened. "What?" She leaned over my shoulder, watching me.

I continued digging through the drawers to see what else I could find when I came across an old journal with no lock or key on it. I was about to open it when I heard the creak of the door hinges.

In unison, our heads swiveled toward the door. It moved on its own as though a gust of wind whooshed through the hallway. I stopped and listened. The hallway was quiet. "Okay, guys, I don't want to freak you out or anything, but this place is starting to creep me out," Bear said.

"Starting to?" Jay asked, sneering at Bear. He shrugged in reply.

There was another gust of wind, and the sound of a voice, sounding far away, came in from the window. "Help! Someone help me!" The voice got closer and more desperate. "Help! Please!"

Bear pointed his flashlight at the broken window. It sounded like the voice was coming from above us. Maybe the roof. Jay stood there frozen with horror written on her face. *Who could be out there?* I wondered.

I straightened from my crouch and began backing toward the door, still clutching the journal in my hand. "We should go, guys."

Bear turned the flashlight back on me, and I could see a cloud of my breath in front of me. My teeth chattered in response.

"Dude," Bear said, "the temperature just dropped like thirty degrees. It's freezing in here." He held out his hand and felt the air in the room.

With a sudden bang, the door slammed shut, making me jump out of my skin.

"What's going on?" said Jay as she moved closer to me. "Why is it so cold?"

Bear answered for me. "I think we're dead." The flashlight beam grew brighter for a moment, giving us one quick moment of light before flickering off.

There was a scream, and again, it sounded like it was coming from above. I heard Jay whimper, and I felt my hand shake as I reached for her. The air grew even colder, and my teeth chattered. I clutched Jay's hand, trying to tell myself that this was some kind of prank, but I didn't believe it. There was another scream, and it echoed through the room like a shuddering giant. Jay released my hand to cover her ears, and I did the same. We huddled close together for warmth.

I was about to suggest we try to break the door down when it swung open, revealing a small window of light from outside the building. Bear ran through first with me close behind him, pulling Jay along beside me. We moved as fast as we could through the threshold of the classroom.

I sensed something reaching out of the darkness to grasp at me but ran faster. Zach was the last through the door, which slammed shut on its own right behind him. I jumped at the sound of wood cracking with brutal force. Our heavy breathing was the only sound in the empty corridor. I glanced around the hallway to see if anything followed or greeted us.

"What the heck was that?" Bear asked, glancing at us one at a time. "Did you guys see that? Tell me you all saw that."

"What was with you saying we're dead?" Zach asked, anger bubbling up beneath the surface. He shined the flashlight down the hallway in one direction and then in the other. There was nothing with us in the hall. "Let's get back to the gym," Zach said.

"Let's try the windows," Jay said. "Maybe we can get out from this level." The boys looked at her like it hadn't occurred to them to leave, but I nodded and followed her into the nearest classroom on the backside of the building.

One window was boarded up, and the rest were intact, but at the far end of the room, one window had no glass remaining. Jay walked over to it, and I followed. The boys stopped at the entrance, glancing back in the hallway to see if anything approached. Jay leaned over the windowsill and looked down.

"Can you make the jump?" I asked from behind her.

Jay glanced at me over her shoulder. "Easy," she said, but there was doubt in her eyes. I wanted to tell her not to risk it, but this had all gotten too serious. Travis was missing. Something supernatural was happening.

Jay rested her hands on the ledge and swung one leg up on the sill. Her toe caught the edge. Catlike, she lifted her other leg and perched on all fours, glancing at the darkness below. "I can't really see what's down there, but it doesn't look like anything."

I edged closer to the window as Jay swung out her legs and sat on the windowsill. She said, "Dude, what if there's a fence or something?"

I moved over, placing the journal on the floor and pointing the flashlight at her landing zone. "It looks clear from here, but you don't have to do this," I said.

She sat with her legs dangling and her weight back on her hands. Her fingers clenched the ledge, and she pushed herself up. I could hear her breathing faster as she straightened her body out, her butt moving off the ledge. She looked at me, and I nodded.

She tried to lower herself, but her descent halted. "I can't move. I can't let go," she said, grimacing with her struggle. At first, I thought it was because she was scared.

I held out my hand and took a step forward. "Give me your hand, and I'll pull you back up."

She winced, her face contorting in pain. "I can't! My hand is stuck!"

I reached forward and grabbed her wrist so that if she did let go, she wouldn't fall. I tried to tug her hand free, but it was stuck fast, as though the wood had grown into her skin, rooting her to the window. Jay looked at me, her eyes wide with fear. "Help!" she shouted, her voice echoing in the empty room. She kicked her legs up and was once again seated on the ledge, but her hands held fast to the wood. I tried to pull back on her. I could feel the tendons in her wrist straining, but she wouldn't let go.

I heard a noise and looked over my shoulder. Bear and Zach stood behind me, uncertain of what to do. There was a howling noise from deep in the school, more like a demented cry of some lamenting soul.

"Help me, Sam! It hurts!" she called again.

The noise grew louder. Someone, or something, was coming. I reached my arm around Jay's waist and pulled back, leaning with all of my weight. There was a moment of resistance before we both tumbled back. I held Jay, and Bear and Zach caught the both of us, like some kind of team trust fall.

I helped Jay back to her feet as she held her hands in front of her. The skin on her palm was scraped raw, and blood coated her fingers. "What the hell?" I muttered as I examined her injury.

"It won't let us leave," she whispered as Bear and Zach ushered us into the hallway, but not before I grabbed the journal and clasped it against my chest. Jay's eyes were wide as she stared off into the distance. There was another banshee wail, but this time, it was closer. "What was that?" she asked.

"Maybe it's better if we don't know," said Bear, his hands clenched into fists at his sides.

There was a sound from behind us, and I turned around to see an old woman coming toward us. She was dressed in a long white gown, yellowed with age and the hem lined with dirt. Her skin mottled and gray—she looked like a walking corpse. My mouth dropped open, but something trapped the words in my throat and took my breath away.

"You belong to him now," she whispered in a raspy voice as she raised a hand toward us. "I tried to warn you, but you're his." Her hollow eyes glowed, and the flesh on her face drooped like melted wax.

Jay screamed as Zach yanked us away from the woman. "Come on! Let's go!" Bear was the first back down the hall, running past Zach and Jay toward the gym.

Flashlights shone here and there, creating a disorienting strobe effect. I stumbled multiple times, every time righting myself before I landed on my face. I bumped into Jay as I turned into the hallway, and she'd tripped over some leftover debris. Zach turned around and grabbed Jay by the elbow, but her legs tangled together, and she fell hard onto the hallway floor. His eyes widened at her as he tried to lift her up, but she was still on the ground. I grabbed her other arm and hoisted her up from the floor.

"Come on!" Bear yelled. "We're almost there."

The guys took off ahead of us, and I could see the gym door open up ahead. I could hear Jay's panting breath as she ran beside me, trying to keep up with our pace.

We made it back to the center court on the gym floor, gasping for breath. My heart was beating so hard it pounded in my ears and echoed in my brain. We huddled together under the lone light in the gym. It gave off a false sense of security, but I was grateful for it.

As I looked around at the eyes of my friends, only one met my gaze. Zach opened his mouth to speak, but Bear beat him to it. "That was no projector," he said.

Chapter 15

As we settled in a circle on the gym floor, I placed the journal in my lap, running my hand over the cracked leather cover. I had to find out what was behind the cover, no matter what. There might be answers inside. I flipped to a random page. The well-worn pages were soft, and the binding felt fragile. The entries were written in several colors of ink, but each word was formed with the same elegant cursive script. The ink had faded, leaving some of the words illegible.

"You still have that thing?" Jay asked, and I looked up, realizing that everyone was watching me.

I nodded. "Why wouldn't I?" I felt the grooves of the sentences flowing across the pages.

"Should you be reading that?" Bear asked. "She seemed pretty pissed at us."

I shrugged and looked at Bear. "There's only one way to find out." Slowly, I turned the pages of the book. "I don't think it's her we have to worry about," I answered. "She said, 'you belong to him now' so I don't think she's the one who took Travis." I eyed Zach. "You don't still think Travis is in on this, do you?"

"I don't know what I think or what I saw." Zach put his head in his hands and rubbed his temples.

"But you're not really supposed to be reading it," Bear said. His brown hair was a mess on top of his head. "It's not right. It's private." If we weren't in this situation, I'd laugh at Bear's sincerity.

The smell of mold tickled my nose, so I breathed through my mouth. "I think she wanted us to read it," I said. "I think that noise led us to the room." Everything was quiet except for the fluttering of those dry old pages. On some pages, it was hard to make sense of the words because there were deep gouges in the pages, slashing the remnants of words out of existence.

"What about the journal?" Jay said, leaning closer to me. "What does that say?"

"I can't really tell." I flipped through the pages. "Parts of it are all hacked up. Someone went crazy on it with a knife or something." I flipped back to the beginning. "Some of it is just worn out."

As I looked up, I caught Zach and Bear exchanging a subtle glance.

"Well, let me see." Jay grabbed the book out of my hands and squinted at the destroyed pages. "Hey!" she yelled, pointing at an unscarred chunk of text, and read out loud. "May twenty-third. Theo Lobel. Who would have thought? When we were in high school, he never would have noticed me. Now, I have the attention of the hottest man in town. I've seen Katie at the bank studying me, trying to decide whether I'm worthy of her ex. I don't care. Theo Lobel told me he loved me, and nothing could ever make me happier."

Jay turned the journal to face us. There were hearts doodled all over the pages. On the bottom, in the faintest ink, she signed it, Mona Lobel.

"Wow. She had it bad." Jay let out a whistle, tracing Mona's practice signature.

"I don't think this is anything to joke about," Bear said, glancing around at the rest of the dark gym. Bear was the joker, so the fact he was taking this seriously made my stomach churn.

"What else does it say?" I asked, leaning closer.

Jay squinted at the book and flipped to the middle of the journal. "October twelfth, Theo was angry again tonight. He tried to read my journal, so now I'm keeping you at work, which isn't the safest place. He just gets so jealous, and sometimes I like it because then I know he cares." Jay looked up at us. "Wait, that's messed up. She liked it when he got jealous?" We glanced at each other in uncomfortable silence.

"Keep reading," I said. Jay eyed me and glared back at the pages.

"October thirteenth, Theo came home late last night all scratched up and bleeding, so angry and so amped up on something. He had a knife in his hand, but he didn't do anything with it. I fear him when he's like this." Jay looked up at me and handed the book back. "I can't read any more."

I stared at the pages, careful not to let my hands shake. "Do you think he did something to her?"

It was Zach's turn to say, "Keep reading."

I flipped the page, running my fingers down the text as though it was written in braille. "October sixteenth, Theo came home last night drunk. He couldn't tell me where he was. He told me he loved me, but his hands were trembling. I haven't seen him this bad since that night on May third."

Zach looked up at me again. "What's May third?"

"I don't know. I'd have to look back," I said, ready to flip to the front of the journal.

"No," Jay said, "keep reading." I glanced over at Bear, staring at the hidden door with his hands over his ears.

"October eighteenth. I finally got Theo to sleep last night. He cried like he was afraid he was going to lose me. He's done with that junk now, but he seems different. Scarier."

Jay touched my knee, and I lowered the journal to my lap. "I don't want you to read anymore." Bear nodded in agreement.

Zach spoke. "We need to. There could be clues to what's going on."

I stared at him. This was his first admission that something supernatural was taking place. I took a deep breath before reading, "October nineteenth, I woke up in the middle of the night, and I saw him standing over me, watching me sleep. He wasn't fighting his demons anymore. They were all gone, but he was still scared." Theo

Lobel sounded like a madman, but I wondered how much of the monster was created by Mona's mind games.

Bear stood up and started pacing back and forth next to me. "This isn't what she wrote, right? I mean, she said nothing about what happened to her." He clasped his hands together but didn't stop moving.

I continued, fueled by Bear's frantic energy. "October twentieth. I know what he did now. He tells me all the time, but I can finally see it in his eyes when he looks at me." I felt the fear in those words and thought about what she must have been going through at the time. Afraid to leave the man she once loved, but also afraid of the monster he'd become. "October twenty-first. They're all afraid of him. They tell me to leave him alone, but I never will." I picked up the journal and held it tight against my chest. I wiped tears with the back of my sleeve. I didn't even realize I was crying.

"He did something." Bear sat on the other side of me and stared at the floor. "He didn't just hurt her—he killed her."

"Not necessarily," Jay said. "We don't know that. She could have left him after that."

I shook my head. "I don't think so. I think she stayed because she loved him—even though he was a monster." I held the journal out. "Look. She says all these things about him but never really reveals anything for fear that someone will find the journal. Even her journal isn't private."

Zach and Bear both nodded, and we stared silently at each other for a few minutes. There was a whistling wind coming through one of the broken windows, and I glanced out of the corner of my eye to see the shadow of something moving across the mezzanine.

I gasped at the sight of Mona Desden, her hair nearly floating around her head as though she was underwater. My breath caught, and I felt the hair on my forearms stand straight up. The room grew colder.

"What is it?" Jay asked, but as her eyes followed mine, she sucked in deeply. The boys' gaze traveled to the ghost of Ms. Desden.

"Holy crap!" Bear yelled, jumping up and back away. As Ms. Desden's head slowly turned to face us, I saw her eyes were hollow sockets. She raised and pointed her crooked finger at me, but it wasn't me she was pointing to. It was her journal.

I relaxed my grip on the book, ready for something bad to happen. I got up from the gym floor, and something fell from the book, fluttering to the warped wooden floor.

Zach leaned over and picked it up. It was folded like a note. He unfolded it just as Jay let out a gasp.

"She's gone," Jay said, pointing, and we looked back to where the spirit had been, but she was gone now.

"What was that?" Bear asked, though the answer was obvious.

Zach held the yellowed page that had fallen from the book.

"What is it?" I asked Zach, feeling safer that we were on the gym floor rather than wandering around the school with the vengeful spirits from the past.

"It's a note from someone named Casey Nabs." He straightened it out, reading the words. "Dear Mona, thank you for your kindness and your mentorship. New towns can be unkind, especially to people like me, who are different. I want to thank you for keeping my personal life to yourself." He turned it around so we could see. "That's all it says. It's signed Casey Nabs."

"Who's that?" Bear asked. Zach shrugged in reply.

"He must have worked here," I said. Mona wanted me to find the note. It had to be why she called us to the journal. There was more to her story, and she wanted us to know. An idea hatched in my brain. "There's one way we can find out."

"What's that?" Zach asked, and I could tell he really didn't want to know.

I spoke slowly. "We could see if there are any yearbooks left in the library." Three pairs of eyes stared blankly at me.

Jay shook her head. "Are you crazy? I'm not going up there."

"No one is," Bear said. "We're not leaving the gym."

"Guys, I don't think Mona will stop until we find the answers." I moved in front of Jay, grabbing her hand and holding up her scratched palm. "And there's no way out of here."

Jay closed her fist and stared at the ground, refusing to make eye contact. No one spoke, and just when I was ready to go on my own, Zach stepped closer to me.

"I'll go with you," Zach said. Bear raised an eyebrow as if to say, are you sure? He handed Zach the flashlight.

I turned to Jay and handed her the journal. She gripped it with both hands. "We'll be right back," I said.

"Don't say that," Jay scolded me. "Sam, think about this. You're going up there on the mere chance that there's a yearbook? What if this Casey Nabs doesn't even matter? You're risking your life for nothing." Her eyes were pleading, scared.

"You don't know that," I said to Jay. "If we all want to make it out of here, we have to do something, and I will not sit here until the next one of us is taken."

"But Travis wandered away. If we stick together, we'll be okay." Jay's words were hopeful, but there was no assurance behind them.

I placed my hand on Jay's shoulder. I'd never seen her this frightened. "I know you want to believe that, but the longer we're here, the more we've seen. We've still got hours to go. If we want to make it through the night, we have to do something."

Jay nodded, but something in her eyes told me she didn't believe me. I tried to walk calmly across the gym floor. The wind howled through the cavernous gym, giving me goosebumps. I held onto my arms and tried to ignore the dark corners and the broken windows that looked into blackness.

Chapter 16

Once Zach and I left the gym floor, we didn't hesitate. We ran up the steps and across the mezzanine without stopping to see if any spirits or angry ghosts gave chase. I wasn't looking for another run-in with Mona Desden.

We made it to the next flight of stairs. "I think the library is on the third level," I said, pointing down the hall. "I saw the entrance when we were up here earlier." Zach nodded, his mouth a grim line.

The library was just around the corner. I could see the long hallway ending in double doors. This part of school looked worse for the wear. Fallen beams littered the hallway, and we avoided pieces of plaster that covered the floor, ducking under obstacles and weaving our way into more darkness.

We took our time making our way through the corridor to the library. Every fiber of my being begged me not to go in there, but we'd come this far, and I wasn't about to give up now.

We pushed open the double doors and stood on the precipice of the room. There was a desk with a stack of moldy books on it and a stack of boxes against a wall so covered in mildew and dust they looked ancient. Zach stepped sideways into the room and over to the boxes, picking up a musty book from one of them. Spiderwebs clung to the water-stained book cover, and he switched hands, wiping the grit on his shirt.

Tossing the book down, he turned his flashlight to the far side of the room. Old Encyclopedias and dictionaries stacked the shelves on the east wall. "That looks like the reference section," I said, excited. I moved over to Zach's side and peered over his shoulder.

Something groaned in the walls as a warning. Zach pointed the flashlight up to the ceiling and the shattered skylight. He brought the flashlight to the floor, illuminating the rotted and warped floorboards. As he brought the flashlight closer to where we stood, there was a large hole in the floor, and exposed beams and other debris with jagged edges lay beneath the gaping wound. I wondered how long it had been exposed to the weather. This entire room probably wasn't safe to walk in.

"I think you should go wait in the hallway," he said, his voice low.

"You want me to leave you alone in here?" I asked, placing my hands on my hips.

He said nothing at first, but when I grabbed his arm, and he turned to me. "We don't know how much of this building is rotted. This could be dangerous."

"I'm not leaving you alone," I said.

A fallen beam lay on the floor near us and it created a bridge across the open space about five feet wide. There was no way to get across the hole without walking on the beam. As I stepped on the beam and tested it with my weight, it seemed sturdy enough. I suddenly realized how high up we were, and if we slipped and fell through, there would be nothing but concrete and jagged, rough wood and metal below us.

"I could jump it," Zach said. "But what about you?" I looked at him. For a split second, he blushed just the tiniest bit, and then his face turned serious again.

We'd need to traverse the hole in the floor to get to the yearbooks. "This is stupid," I said. "Maybe we should just go back. We don't even know if the yearbooks are over there, much less the right one."

Zach inched away from the door and closer to the warped spot on the floor. He shined the flashlight down, studying the wooden floor. The light from the flashlight shined back at us, broken into little pieces by the shattered glass that covered everything around us. The beam looked solid enough. There were no cracks or mold on it.

"I think it's safe to walk on," he said.

He held out his arm and motioned for me to go ahead of him. "You're lighter than me. You go first, and I'll follow."

"Thanks. At least you're not thinking of me as some frail girl."

"That's not what I meant," Zach started, but I raised my hand, stopping him. I didn't like that idea, but he was right that if one of us fell through the floor, the other might help him. I also appreciated that he didn't pull the man's card.

I took a step onto the beam, and my shoe held firm. The next few steps were slow, and I was waiting for the floor to give way or the beam to crack. But the floor held, and I made it to the other side. Zach followed, not as graceful as me, but he made it across the beam safely.

"We need to go around that side," he said, pointing with the flashlight toward the reference section. I was hesitant to take another step, but he wasn't. He moved around the warped spot and headed toward the yearbooks. I followed behind him closely, praying that the floor wouldn't give way.

We reached our destination, and I let out a sigh of relief when my feet didn't go crashing through the floor. We moved on to the reference section of the library, and there they were. The yearbooks. They were dusty and stained with water damage. The pages inside were moist but still held their form.

There were three yearbooks sitting on top of a pile of other books and papers. Zach grabbed the one in the middle, and I watched him page through it while muttering Casey Nabs under his breath.

A noise came from somewhere inside the library, and I stopped. He stopped, and we both listened. The noise came again, and I realized it was the sound of someone whistling.

Zach turned to me, but he didn't make a sound. It took him a moment to pull himself together. He opened another box of old books on the desk, using his flashlight to scan the staff photo section.

"What do you see?" I asked. He shined the flashlight along the bottom beneath each picture and then looked up at me. "The school was founded in nineteen—whatever." Great, I thought, we still had to find our year.

"If we can't find it, there's a box over there that should have the yearbooks for this decade," he said, nodding toward another corner of the library. "We'll start with those and move forward until we find out."

I went over and started thumbing through the first book. It had class photos starting in the nineteen-sixties.

"What about this one?" I asked, holding out a photo of students lined up in front of the auditorium stage. "What are they wearing?"

He laughed and came over to me. His hand brushed against my back as he leaned down to look at the book. "I don't think that's a school picture," he said, straightening up and stepping back from me.

"It looks like it could be." I took another look at the pictures of students wearing costumes and laughing as they moved through their paces during an activity instead of standing still for a formal photo.

"I think it's for a play," he said, taking the book from me. His fingertips brushed against mine. My pulse raced as I watched him flip through the yearbooks with me close behind, looking for clues.

He stepped back, turning to me. "Let's try this one," he said and came toward me again and brushed up against my arm as he reached for the book I'd just set down.

I gasped. My heart raced, and I wasn't sure if it was from Zach's closeness or the adrenaline pumping through my body.

"This is it," he said, pointing at a picture of Mona Desden. "She's here." He skimmed the page and tapped his finger on another picture. It was a young man with blond hair and boyish curls. "Bingo!" he yelled. "Casey Nabs. We found the right yearbook," he said. His face was close to mine, and I caught a whiff of his cologne mingled with wood smoke. He looked into my eyes, and warmth flooded through me as I realized how much I enjoyed being this close to him.

"Bring it with," I said, before turning away from him. "We'll search for clues back down in the gym."

"Good thinking," he said, backing up. He bumped into the desk and dropped his flashlight, which clattered to the floor and flickered like it might go out. "Damn," he called out, bending over to grab it. We wouldn't be able to traverse the beam without the flashlight.

A gust of wind blew in from the broken skylight, and I remembered before when the room got cold. I moved closer to Zach, bumping into him. He stood, his shoulder brushed against mine, and electricity shot through me.

His breathing grew heavy, and he said, "Got it. Let's go." His eyes locked with mine, and I felt something inside me shift. Everything else seemed to fade away—the school, the ghosts, my fears—they all dissolved, leaving only Zach and me.

His breath caught as though he read my mind. It felt like the room grew hazy with smoke, and Zach's lips were moving, but his voice didn't sound like his own. "I really like you," he said. "I can't think about anyone else but you."

My heart stopped, and I stared at him. He leaned closer to me until our lips were almost touching. "I love you," he said, lowering his mouth to mine and kissing me softly. His lips fit perfectly against mine, and I closed my eyes, letting everything else fade away. He put a hand on my hip and pulled me closer to him until I felt his chest press against me.

He broke away from the kiss and looked into my eyes. "I'm sorry," he said. "I didn't mean to. I shouldn't have just kissed you. I don't know what came over me." He was panting.

"Don't apologize." I pulled him back against me. I could feel his heart thumping wildly in his chest.

A loud clap of thunder echoed through the building, and Zach jerked back from me. There was a crack as his foot broke through the floor. I was still holding him when he fell backward, and I tightened my grip, grunting with effort.

He dropped the yearbook and caught himself with one hand while gripping the flashlight with the other. I yanked at his shirt again, and he pulled his leg free from the craggy floorboards, rolling over onto his hands and knees.

"Holy shit!" he yelled. I moved over to his side, helping him up from the floor. "That was close," he said. My tongue was too numb to form words, so I reached down and scooped up the yearbook. "Come on," he said as he grabbed my free hand. "We need to find out what

Casey Nabs has to say." I stared at him for a moment, my brain replaying that moment differently, watching Zach plummet through the flooring. Tears threatened me. My feelings were jumbled. I took a step back and bumped into the table behind me. My hands were shaking.

"Let's go," he said. "Let me lead the way this time," Zach said, handing over the flashlight in exchange for the yearbook. The light shook with my hand, and we followed the same path on our way out, only this time, I clenched my teeth, watching each of Zach's steps.

Then, smoke billowed in the light of the flashlight, and I breathed it in, coughing while almost losing my balance. Flames erupted around us, and with my free arm, I attempted to shield myself from the bright glow of the fire. I dropped the flashlight, and it hit the beam before spinning wildly through the hole in the floor, clanking on various materials as it plummeted below us. I reached for Zach to steady myself.

"What's going on?" I screamed. The crackle of the flames and groaning of the building muffled my voice as the acrid ashes coated my tongue.

"I don't think it's real," Zach called over his shoulder, maintaining his balance, but I felt the searing heat from every side. The flames reached up and licked the ceiling. "Keep going," Zach called.

Zach reached an arm back toward me until his hand hung in the air. I moved forward, letting him help me across the narrow wooden beam. I tried to ignore the sweat dripping from my brow as my lungs screamed from lack of clean oxygen.

Zach stepped off the beam first and pulled me the rest of the way to him, still walking gingerly on the warped wooden floor. We backed to the door together, watching the flames consume the room, but when we stepped back to the double doors, there was a whoosh of cold air. I blinked at it was gone. The flames. The smoke. The room was as it was when we first entered.

"What the hell was that?" Zach asked, looking back at me, though it was difficult to see him in the dark after being blinded by those reaching flames. I'd lost the flashlight, so we'd have to make it back to the gym in the dark.

"I think someone didn't want us to get our hands on the yearbook," I said, with a nervous sensation in my gut. My palms were sweaty, and I wiped them on my pants. My stomach was in knots.

Zach moved closer to me and put a hand on my back. "That means we're on the right track," he said. "Don't be scared. It'll all work out."

But I knew he was just saying that. He didn't know what was going to happen any more than I did. "I hope so," I said, glancing back at him and taking his hand in mine. He handed me the yearbook and began guiding me down the hallway, squeezing my hand as we felt our way through the long, dark corridor.

Chapter 17

Our trip back down to the gym was uneventful, and when we returned, Jay ran to meet us. "We've gone over the journal, and I don't believe Mona did anything. I don't think she cheated," Jay said, her voice rising with delight. She lowered her gaze to my hand. "You found the yearbook! Is he in there?"

"Yes," I said. "We found Casey Nabs, but we didn't have time to look through the yearbook." I looked at Zach, wondering how much we were going to tell Jay and Bear. They were freaked out, and I didn't want them any more frightened than they already were.

"Yeah," Zach agreed. "The library is falling apart. There's an enormous hole in the floor." Zach's mouth clamped shut.

Bear noticed Zach's abrupt silences. "Did anything happen when you were there?"

As Zach shook his head from side to side, I felt my cheeks flush. Jay's gaze scorched a hole in me. I knew Bear was talking about angry spirits, and I should have been thinking about the ghostly fires, but my thoughts traveled back to the kiss. I couldn't figure out what came over us.

Zach broke the tense quiet. "Can you tell me what you found in the journal?"

"Oh," Bear said. "We think this Casey guy was gay."

"That's the only plausible answer," Jay said, holding out the journal as proof.

Zach's forehead furrowed in confusion. "What exactly do you mean?"

"How do you know that?" I asked.

"It's what he said in his note and the rest of Mona's journal entries we got through about them being such close friends," Jay said.

"So, what if he's gay?" Zach asked.

Jay rolled her eyes. "Think about it," she said. "He's gay, and Mona really liked him. She mentions Casey dated very little because he was probably afraid of coming out to his friends. Theo thinks Casey only has eyes for her."

"So?" Zach asked again. I couldn't help but look at Jay, though I didn't want to give her away. Her face was turning red. Zach didn't know what he was doing to her, but it wasn't helping my frustration. She played it cool, but sometimes the looks and comments from others got to her.

Jay continued. "Small town like this? You know there'd be some parents who'd complain to the school board about this 'alternative lifestyle.'" She used her fingers to mime air quotes.

"Could they do that?" Bear asked.

"They still can in some places," I said. "There's a football player at Littleford who came out, and his parents pulled him from the team."

"I think you'd be surprised." Jay made eye contact before averting her gaze.

"Isn't Smelly from Littleford?" Bear asked.

Then it dawned on me. The secret about Travis that Jay mentioned earlier. I wonder if Travis was the Littleford football player.

Jay continued. "Mona had to have known he was gay."

"So, what happened that night?" Zach asked.

The sudden realization saturated my thoughts like a tsunami rushing over me. I forced a swallow. I didn't want to believe that Mona would cheat on Theo. It was most likely my own guilt that I was experiencing. "Theo, her husband. He must have assumed Mona was deceiving him." I cast a peek at Zach.

Zach's eyes widened. "The shouting we heard on the roof," he said. "They were arguing. Maybe they both tripped during the altercation? Maybe they jumped?"

I continued, "Who can say? But Mona wasn't having an affair with Casey. She was shielding him." I examined each face. "I bet Theo was the one who killed Casey, and he came back to take his revenge on Mona."

"I knew this place was haunted!" Bear yelled, and at the same time, the basement door flew open, banging against the wall like gunfire in the still night.

"What the hell?" Zach threw his hand out in front of me to shield me. Jay put her hands up to cover her ears, dropping the journal.

Nothing happened as the door ricocheted off the wall and, in a slow arc, stopped halfway open. "Who's there?" Bear yelled.

Seconds passed, and I gradually noticed the faint sound of music being played on a vehicle stereo in the distance.

I couldn't speak when I noticed that in the dim light, it looked like a figure stood behind Jay.

Jay stared at her shaking hands before glancing up at me and following my gaze. She turned her head to face the shadows and screamed as a figure lunged at her, knocking her to the side like a rag doll.

"Bear!" I shouted, willing him to help her. He grabbed Jay's wrist and yanked her up and out of harm's path. As they backed away from the door, I could hear her sobbing.

I moved closer to them. "It's okay, Jay! It's okay, we got your back!" Luckily, my voice worked, and she kept quiet as we watched the shadows move inside the room. Someone was in there with us.

"Who do you think it is? Theo?" Bear whispered, eyes wide as he stared at the pool of darkness, which suddenly shifted and spread out like a ripple in a pond until it filled the width of the doorway and crawled toward us like black water.

The pounding of my heart was matched only by the heavy weight in my stomach, as if I'd swallowed a rock.

As the darkness neared, we heard heavy breathing and slow footsteps approaching the door. We waited, frozen in terror. The smell of smoke and ash filled the room.

"Who is it?" Bear asked. "Show yourself!"

I was still staring at Jay when a figure appeared next to her. The figure's eyes sank into its skull, and his lips were black and peeled apart from the gums as if speaking, but no words came out. There was a hole in his cheek that revealed an empty void beneath the flesh.

"Jay!" I screamed, reaching for her when two rotting, ghostly hands wrapped around her ankles. She let out a guttural grunt, unable to form words. Before anyone could react, Jay was being pulled away from us, dragged across the gym floor.

"Sam!" Jay screamed, clawing at the floor for something to grip. "Sam!"

Bear joined me, running after her. "Jay!" He yelled into the silence that only made me panic more. He passed me, stumbled, leaning over and reaching for Jay's hand.

I watched as she was slowly dragged away from us and into the dark.

"Jay!" I screamed, and I noticed the ghastly figure was wearing singed clothing like he'd survived a fire, but the clothes looked a lot like what Travis was wearing earlier. The figure vanished out of sight first and then Jay right after.

Bear stumbled forward, and I noticed the edge of darkness ripple, like a black tide ready to swallow Bear whole.

"Bear, stop!" I yelled at him, but he ran after her, disappearing into the darkness of the gym floor with Jay screaming his name above the pounding of footsteps and heavy breathing.

"Bear!" I screamed and ran after them, leaving Zach behind me.

"Sam, wait!" he yelled after me, but I couldn't stop myself from running into the darkness, even though it felt like I was being pulled apart by an invisible force.

As we ran out of the gym, the wooden basketball court beneath our feet gave way to the rough, cold cement floor.

"Jay!" I screamed as I rounded the corner of the hallway, but I skidded to a halt when I came to my senses. Jay was gone, but Bear stood alone, searching in the darkness.

"Jay!" I yelled, turning around in a circle, searching for my friend. There were no footprints in the dust and debris. No trail of a dragging body. It was as though she'd vanished. "What do we do? Where's Jay?" My voice echoed off the building walls.

"She's gone," Zach said from behind me. I didn't even hear him catch up to us.

"No," Bear whispered beside me, shaking his head. "No," he said louder. "We gotta get out of here." He turned to Zach, grabbing him by the shoulders. "We gotta get out of here!" His eyes were wide.

"We're not going anywhere," I said. Zach and Bear turned to look at me. "There's no getting out of here. We have to figure out who didn't want us to have the yearbook. We have to find Jay and Travis. We owe it to them."

Zach gave a nod. "We do, yes." He turned to face Bear. "Come on, man! We need to find them before it's too late. You know that."

Bear paused for a second longer, then gave a nod and took off running down the hallway in the only direction Jay could have gone.

Zach's eyes darted towards me for a moment before he took off in pursuit. With a frustrated growl, I followed behind them. We ran through the winding corridors, the sound of our footsteps echoing off the walls. My head was spinning, and I felt disoriented. We didn't run into any fires or ghosts, but we also weren't getting anywhere. There was no sign of Jay.

Bear led us through a labyrinth of corridors on the first floor until we had completed a full circle. As we approached the gym, Bear's legs gave out beneath him, and he crumpled to the floor in tears.

"What are you doing?" Zach asked.

Bear struggled to gather his breath and standing. He shook his head anxiously as he backed away from us toward the gym entrance. "This has to be some kind of sick joke. This can't be real, you guys."

"It's real, Bear," Zach said, his voice low and calming, but it didn't matter. The expression on Bear's face told me he'd been here long enough to have fully lost it, and there was no space for logic in his head.

Chapter 18

B ear remained collapsed in the corridor outside the gym. He sobbed softly into his palms. I placed a hand on his shoulder. "It's all right," I murmured calmly. "We're here for you. It's okay."

He shook his head, brushing his hair away from his face. "No, it's not okay," he answered emphatically. "Jay's gone. Travis is gone. One of us is next." He motioned around the vacant corridor. "This place killed them all," he said, peering off into the distance.

My cheeks flushed with rage. "They're not dead," I said. I couldn't let him think that because then it might be true. Jay was the toughest person I had ever met. I wouldn't even entertain the thought.

"Come on. Get up," Zach said harshly, grabbing him by the arm.

Bear looked at him in shock. "What?"

"We aren't done searching the school!" Zach snapped. He turned on a flashlight he'd held. I didn't even understand where it had come from.

"It's no use. She's gone," Bear said. "Let's just go back to the gym." He looked toward the stairs that led to the gym. The light was visible from around the corner.

"The gym isn't safe anymore," Zach said. "There are no safe places here." Zach's voice rose, and I could see Bear's chin quivering.

I put a hand on Bear's shoulder to calm him. "He's right," I said, trying to keep my voice steady. "We need to find Jay and Travis. Are you with us?"

Bear nodded grimly and stood, pressing out the wrinkles in his shirt.

"Okay," I said, rubbing my eyes. "Let's go."

The two guys followed me as I stepped further into the darkness. "Jay!" I called down the empty hallway. I knew it felt hopeless, but I couldn't give up on my best friend. We walked away from the gym using Zach's flashlight to guide us.

"They couldn't just disappear," Zach said, but even his words sounded doubtful. Anything could happen at this point.

"Maybe they're in on this whole thing," Bear said, his voice sounding hopeful.

"We're not back on that again, are we?" I said, stopping in front of a classroom. "And Jay would never. Jay!" I yelled again, peering through the empty classroom door.

The silence was a void, swallowing our words. Then, there was a fluttering like sheets on a clothesline, and I thought I heard a voice whisper my name.

"I can hear something," I said. "It sounds like—" I waited for the noise to get louder. Then there were voices coming from where we'd just been, by the front entrance. "It's the loop. I think it's starting again."

Both Zach and Bear stared at me like they didn't know what I was saying. I turned too quickly, knocking over a small table by the doorway. The stack of ancient books on top of it collapsed and crashed to the ground. One book landed, opened, and I looked down at it.

Zach grasped me by the shoulder as I leaned over to pick up the book. "What are you doing?" he asked. "What were you talking about?"

I returned my gaze to him before leaning back over and taking the book into my hands, feeling the weight of it.

"What is it?" Zach asked. Bear was still staring at the door.

I chewed my lip before speaking. "Remember, Mr. Zimbo talking about Othello?" I asked.

"No," Zach said, shaking his head. Then I remembered the note. Zach probably had heard nothing during that class.

"Well," I said, thinking back to Othello. "Theo murdered his fiancée in a jealous passion from some idea planted in his head. Only it was Mona who put that idea there. Anyway, maybe something trapped their spirits in this place." I set the book back on the table. "And now they're trapped in some kind of loop."

Bear actually looked calm when he asked, "So, what happened to that creepy chick? Why is she upset with us if her boyfriend murdered her? What did we do?"

Bear's words sunk in. He was right. There was something more to the story. Something we were missing. "Maybe, over time, the spirits lose it. Maybe they get frustrated with their situation. I'd probably go crazy being murdered night after night." Then, a thought occurred to me. If the spirit of Theo murdered Mona because he thought she cheated, then maybe Zach and I had angered him when we kissed. Maybe it reawakened the feelings all over again. Could that be enough to anger Mona, too? I didn't share my thoughts because I didn't want to admit in front of Bear that Zach and I had kissed. But why would the spirits be mad at Travis and Jay? It was all too confusing. And what was with Casey Nabs?

The sound down the hall grew louder. They must be on the move. I wanted to follow them but didn't want to risk angering them.

"All we have to do is stick together," Zach said, as though reading my mind.

"That didn't work out all that well for Jay," Bear said, his eyes traveling from Zach and then to me. He looked at his feet, ashamed at his outburst.

In the distance came a voice calling, "Theo, no!" The voices were coming from above us now. We looked at each other, and Zach reached for me before I took off.

"Don't, Sam." He grabbed my wrist.

"That's Mona. I don't think she's dangerous." The air smelled like charred wood, singed hair, and charred flesh. I thought about the fire in the library and wondered if there was a connection. "This is our chance to see what happened." I shook off his hand and dashed up the steps. I felt my chest constrict and my knees creak like old door hinges.

Dust, mud, and grit covered the wide, steep steps. I took them two at a time and was relieved to hear Zach and Bear's footsteps close behind me. I didn't want to split up, but there was no way we were getting out of here without solving the mystery.

The screaming noise that we heard earlier was coming from the roof, so I needed to find the door that led up there. When I reached the third floor, I ran in the opposite direction of the library. It did not matter to me how many doors banged beneath us. I had one goal in mind. At the end of the passageway, a rusty metal door stood, and I glanced back at Zach and Bear, who were right behind me.

"There." I pointed before turning and running. The door was open a crack, and I pushed through to reach a narrow flight of stairs. Moving two steps at a time along the concrete steps was almost claustrophobic. Despite the darkness, the door to the roof was still flapping open, giving glimpses of the streetlights surrounding the school. My adrenaline pushed me forward to catch a breath of fresh night air.

As I made it onto the roof, the door slammed behind me as I rushed to inhale the fresh air. I reached back to grasp the handle, trying to open it, but it was locked.

"Sam!" Zach's voice came from the other side of the door. I heard hammering as I imagined Sam and Bear attempting to smash down the door from the inside.

Voices sounded from the far edge of the roof behind me.

"I did nothing, Theo," said the woman. When I turned around, there stood the spirits of Theo and Mona, but they didn't look like ghosts. It was as though they had come alive.

Chapter 19

They didn't appear to be paying attention to me. Theo wore trousers and a sweater, while Mona's clothes, which were tattered earlier, now transformed into an angelic white dress that fluttered around her in the night breeze. Her face was bone-white, and she had a glow about her that could have been an aura. The night air smelled of dried leaves, roses, mint, and just a hint of leather. Theo was elegant, but Mona transformed into something purer, more beautiful. She was a slow-motion Snow White., and I understood where Theo's jealousy had come from.

"Casey was just a friend." Mona clutched her arms, cold in the night. The air whispered around me, its music luring me in. I wanted to reach out and touch her arm, but there was an invisible barrier between us.

"I saw the way he looked at you," Theo said, his voice slurred. He pointed an angry finger in her direction. "I know you were flirting with him, wanting to get back at me."

"Oh please," Mona said, rolling her eyes and patting his arm dismissively. "You're acting crazy, Theo. He wasn't interested in me in that way. But that doesn't matter anymore, does it? You made sure of it."

"Don't call me crazy," Theo said, his voice rising. "You were keeping a secret with him. I saw it in your journal. Tell me what it is!"

"You really are insane, Theo." Mona's voice trailed off. I could see the fear in her eyes as she watched him pace.

Theo laughed bitterly, threw his hands up into the air, then let them fall limp at his side. "I'm not crazy," he said again, slowly this time, so she could understand. His voice was steady, but his eyes were wild, darting about the place like he was seeing the world in slow-motion. "And I'm not drunk." His words came out slurred and slow.

"What are you doing?" Mona's words came out sharp and clear, slicing through the air like a blade.

"You don't belong with Casey." Theo had thrown his hands up into the air again. This time they stayed there as if he was pleading with God himself. "We are meant to be together. You can see that, can't you?"

"I belong wherever I am," Mona said, her voice more confident now. "You have to see that, too." She reached out her hand and touched his face gently. I couldn't help but think how different she sounded from the girl at the beginning of her journal.

Theo's hands pressed into Mona's middle like he was trying to catch the air that he couldn't hold. His face twisted in slow-motion and tears trailed down his cheeks, shining in the moonlight.

"I can show you how you can be with me." Theo's voice broke. He let his hands drift to her sides, but they drifted back up again, above where he had originally put them. "I can show you how." His arms gently floated out to the side as if he was explaining it to someone else for understanding, then his fingers twitched and grabbed her again. His eyes were watery, and his lips quivered and tightened into a thin line.

"Theo." Mona's voice resonated through me, shaking every atom in my body, sending vibrations through my bones.

Theo didn't hear her. He was too engrossed in his own little world where everything was perfect, where they could be together in a way that made sense to him.

"Theo," Mona said again, her voice echoing through my mind. "You're hurting me." His arms clenched around her tighter. "I love you," she said, her voice desperate for him to understand that he was hurting her. "And I will always be yours."

"Why do you have to hurt me?" he pleaded with her.

"There was only one thing I couldn't tell you. I promised him," she said. "And you had no right to read my journal." I willed her to stop speaking, but she just kept pushing.

"I knew you were keeping secrets from me." He grabbed her by the wrist, dragging her over to the edge of the roof. I covered my mouth to mask my gasp.

"Theo! Stop it," she cried. "You're hurting me!"

"Don't you see?" he snarled through gritted teeth, his grip tightening. "I can't feel anything anymore. You did this to me." He pounded his fist against his chest, punctuating his words.

I jumped in front of him. "Stop!" I yelled, holding up my hands so that he couldn't strike me. "She's telling the truth. She didn't cheat on you."

Theo's eyes widened in surprise as though he'd heard me, but then he turned his attention to Mona, who backed away from him until there was nowhere left to go. He grabbed her by the throat and held her over the edge of the roof. "Did you know I could push just a little harder?" He pushed his hand forward until Mona gasped for air. She clawed at his hand, trying to pull it back and away from her neck.

She peeled his fingertips back, and her weight shifted. Theo's eyes grew wide as she tumbled backward, disappearing into the black void of night.

I felt myself scream as she fell. I felt tears wet on my face as he leaned over the edge and watched her tumble to the ground below and out of sight.

He gasped, reaching out as he looked down. I ran to the side and looked over the edge. There was nothing there, but I knew what he was seeing. The dead body of his fiancée sprawled out across the concrete.

Theo backed up, looking around the empty roof, but when his eyes passed me, he paused for a moment as though seeing me. He gasped, sucking in his final breath, and walked over to the edge, stepping off into the abyss.

"No!" I screamed, reaching for him but knowing what would happen, anyway. As soon as his body made it halfway, he vanished.

The pounding on the door ended as Zach fell through the doorway, stumbling but catching himself before landing on his face. "Sam!" he called. "Are you okay, Sam?" He ran over to the edge and put his arms around me. "Oh my God, Sam. I thought you were dead! I—I saw you fall." He shook his head, tears glistening in the corner of his eyes.

My mouth hung open as the truth dawned on me. "It wasn't me. It was her. They didn't fall. He pushed her, well, accidentally. Then he jumped." I stifled a sob.

"What? Who?" Zach looked around the roof.

"The woman in white. Mona Desden." I glanced back to where they fell.

Zach turned, his eyes wide. "She was here?" He looked around the empty rooftop.

"Yeah, but they're gone now."

"Good," he said, letting out a sigh of relief. He started walking toward the door. "Come on. Let's go back in." All at once, it slammed closed. Zach paused, but there was no wind. I was getting used to doors slamming on their own. Zach threw his body into the door, but it didn't open.

"It's a loop. A death loop. They're reliving the night," I said, watching Zach slump a few inches. He looked exhausted.

"But why?" He leaned his head against the door, his eyes closed. I shrugged, and he slid to the floor. "And what do we have to do with it?"

I sat next to him, putting my hand on his arm. "They didn't fall, but neither of them wanted to die."

"She died because of him. He killed her."

"It was an accident, Zach. They're trapped here because they can't let it go." I looked at his face, and tears welled in my eyes. "They need us to help them find peace."

Zach shook his head, then stood up, taking my hand. "No, Sam. We need to get out of here. There's something else going on here. Something evil."

"We can't get out of here! You know that's why we're here, don't you?" I pleaded with him, but it did no good. "We have to save them!" I screamed.

"No." Zach didn't look at me. "We can't."

I put my hands on my hips and let out a frustrated breath. "I think we started this. The kiss. It was cheating.

I think it woke up Theo, and that's why he's so mad. And poor Mona never cheated. She was just being a good friend."

"We're not cheating, Sam. And Mona was a vindictive. She messed with that poor guy's head." Zach glanced at me out of the corner of his eye. There was a strange tone in his voice.

There was a tapping on the other side of the door. "Hey, guys?" Bear called. "Are you okay?"

Zach stood up and called through the door. "Bear, the door is stuck. Can you open it from your side?"

As I stared at the edge of the roof and then up at the stars in the night sky, a shudder ran through my body. I grumbled in frustration as the door swung open with ease.

Bear was still standing at the top of the stairs, a worried expression on his face. "What exactly is going on?" Bear inquired, his brow furrowed with concern.

"I'm not sure," I mumbled, trying to sound as natural as possible. "But we will figure this out."

Zach marched down the steps in front of us, and I couldn't help but note how his rage mirrored Theo's.

Chapter 20

Zach moved down the hallway toward the stairwell that would bring him to the next landing and then down to the mezzanine level. On the threshold of one room lay a single running shoe—the fabric worn thin. Every time we passed it, I had never noticed it. I felt like I missed something. Or everything.

"Zach, wait!" I called, jogging to catch up to him. He kept his head lowered as he walked. Bear walked a few steps behind, attempting to give us our privacy.

"I don't want to talk about it, okay?" he said over his shoulder. "It's stupid."

"You mean Mona? I think we should—"

He whirled around and shot me a glare that would have curdled milk. "But—" I started, but his expression stopped me short.

His eyes narrowed. "Sam," he said, staring into my eyes. "It's too late for them." His voice wavered, but I could hear the concern.

I shook my head. "No, it's not! We can help them. We can end this!" I said, my voice echoing in the empty hallway.

After swallowing, he looked away for a moment, then back at me. Bear walked to the end of the hallway and stopped, glancing back once before turning his back on us and leaning one shoulder against the wall.

"What's wrong?" I asked, taking a step closer to him. As soon as I placed my hand on his arm, he jerked it away.

"What difference does it make? They're gone, but we're still here. What about our families? If we go missing or die? They'll wonder if they could have done anything to help us when it was all our fault for agreeing to this. What goes on in this school doesn't matter to us any more than what people think of us."

When I glanced at him, I knew exactly what he was thinking. "This isn't about us right now," I said in a low voice.

"Maybe it needs to be. If you think this started because of us, maybe we need to end it." He stared down at me with no hint in his eyes that he was joking.

I didn't want to have this conversation, but I could tell Zach wouldn't cooperate without it. "Zach, you have your plans for the future, and I have mine. I want us to always be friends, but I don't see a way that either of us is going to bend to accommodate each other."

He hesitated for a moment, but his eyes never left mine. "And Bender?" he asked.

I looked away first because I didn't want to see him like this. "Bender is for right now."

"Does he know that?" he asked.

"I don't know," I said, and it was the truth.

"Do you want him to?" His gaze was intense.

I shrugged. "I guess we'll see what happens when we get back." I paused, and he waited for me to continue. "If we get back," I added. I stared at him, realizing for the first time just how heartless I sounded.

He let out a breath and looked away. "You're an idiot." He put his hand on my shoulder for just a moment, then left it there as he started walking again, moving away from me.

I realized he was right. We could die in here, and I was concerned about college and dating someone I could leave behind. Once again, I was so focused on the future that I couldn't see what was in front of me. My hand reached for him and was around his neck as I drew him closer to my face until they were only inches apart.

As his body stiffened and his eyes widened, he never looked away. For a moment, I stared at him, wanting to kiss him so badly that it was killing me not to. "I care about you. If there was nothing else but right now, it would probably change things," I whispered in his ear. "I want you to remember this. Look at me, Zach."

He swallowed hard, and his eyes moved back and forth across my face like he was reading something there. "Sam," he said. "We—"

I kissed him, slow and soft, with everything I had in me because even though I knew it wasn't right, it was what I wanted, and that made it okay.

Zach wrapped his arms around me so tightly my feet left the ground. He turned us slowly, pressing me up against the wall while he kissed me back. I lost myself in him for a moment, a flash of heat running through me as I realized how badly I wanted this.

He suddenly pulled back and looked into my eyes. "Sam," he said before looking away, his face flushed with embarrassment or something else entirely. "Was that just to get me to help you?"

Now my face flushed. "No," I said, but I couldn't explain what had come over me, even though I knew what it looked like. I reached out to him, but he pulled his arm away, turned back toward the stairs.

"Zach!" I called after him, but he didn't stop or look back.

Bear passed me, looking up from under his fringe of hair and shrugging. He picked up his pace to catch up with Zach.

I stood alone in the dark, panting and unsure of what to do next. If I wanted to save my friends, I'd have to stop the loop by myself and quickly. It was my responsibility to them. I looked down the hall, knowing I could get to Mona's room and return in a few minutes before Zach and Bear noticed I wasn't following them.

I ran along the dark hall, my back to the wall, checking behind me every few steps. I arrived at Mona's room in about a minute and stood there for a moment before eventually opening the door.

I inhaled deeply and crossed the threshold. I had no clue what I was going to do or if it would work, but it was the only solution that came to me.

I scanned the room, searching for something that might be useful, and my eyes fell on a few pieces of paper scattered on her desk. I ran over and picked up each piece of paper, studying them one at a time.

The first was a drawing of two people holding hands in the back of a boat. I flipped it over, but there was nothing on the other side, so I put it down and picked up another.

This one had a detailed sketch of someone standing in front of a fireplace. It shocked me to see the drawing was me, dressed nicely and standing in front of a blazing fireplace. There was an elderly woman standing next to me, pointing behind me toward the flames. When I flipped it over, I noticed the initials C.N. on the back. Casey Nabs. He had to have sketched it. When I flipped it back over, the image of myself had changed back to Mona standing next to her mother.

I placed the drawing on Mona's desk, my pulse hammering in my chest. Wind whipped around me, lifting my hair off my shoulders, before vanishing just as fast as it arrived. I had little time to think about what it meant as the sound of heavy footsteps racing down the hall filled the dark room.

Chapter 21

In the hallway, I looked around, but no one was there. I made my way back to the mezzanine because it had the best vantage point. Although I couldn't see the guys on the gym floor, I heard them moving around on the first floor. They were probably checking the windows for an escape route. It wouldn't work. They should have known that by now.

As I stood on the mezzanine, willing Mona to appear, I clenched my hands at my sides. Shaking, I knew none of this would be over until I could figure out how to help the ghosts be at peace.

To my right, something shimmered. Mona Desden appeared in front of me, not in her frightening, zombie-like visage, but in her young, raven-haired form, with an indigo glow illuminating her face. I watched as her hair curled like the petals of a half-opened flower, and her face shone.

I opened my mouth to speak, but she raised an arm, pointing in the distance. Her mouth moved, but the words didn't reach me. Although I felt a scream building in my chest, I didn't want to scare her away again.

Her finger was pointing at the gym floor, and I glanced down before looking back at her. She pointed to the corner where the basement door was. "But there's nothing down there," I said. "We checked." She stared at me with pleading eyes and then looked behind her as though she heard someone approaching.

I didn't know what to do. After another gesture to the gym floor, Mona turned away and floated the length of the mezzanine to the stairs. I knew where she was heading, and I knew she saw Theo following her. They were back in their loop.

While they were busy, I decided I'd check the basement once again. Mona wanted me to see something, and so far, she seemed to be helping me.

I walked down the stairs and stared at center court. Only hours ago, we had all sat in a circle on the warped wooden floor in the gym. Had hours passed since then? A flashlight sat discarded on the floor. I picked it up and clicked it on. Jay's initials were carved on the side of it. I remember her mom had done that one year before summer camp, so no one would take it. I gripped her flashlight with both hands and walked to the open basement door, trying to remember if it had been closed the last time we were down here.

Stepping inside the door, I peered into the darkness. The streetlights from outside still lit up the gym, and with the door open, some of that light reached the basement steps. I took them one at a time, careful to listen for any noises.

When I was halfway down the steps, I heard a thump behind me and spun around. I didn't see anyone, but the door must have been open because it began closing slowly. "No!" I said, running toward it, but it was no use. By the time I got there, the door was already shut. I ran back to it and jiggled the handle, but it wouldn't budge.

I stood there for a second, trying to get my thoughts in order, when something caught my eye at the bottom of the stairwell. A shimmery shadow, like a person, stood below me and I felt my breath catching in my throat. "Mona?" I whispered. I leaned forward, my eyes adjusting to the lack of light. What I saw was nothing like what I expected, though.

The figure at the bottom of the stairs was wearing dress pants and a crisp white button-down shirt, and he was holding something in his hands. "It's okay," he whispered, stepping into the dim light that made it down the stairs. His hair was blond and full of natural curls.

"Are you Casey?" I asked, squinting in the darkness, recognizing his face from the picture in the yearbook. He nodded silently before raising something between us. It was a metal box, and I remember the box from earlier, the one I dropped out of the locker.

"What is it?" I asked.

"Thank you," Casey said. "You set me free." I stared at the box in his hand and looked back up into his ghostly face. His eyes were voids.

"I set you free?" I asked.

He nodded again, still staring at me. He let go of the box. I stood frozen, staring after it as it tumbled end over end through the darkness. My heart was thumping in my chest by the time it hit the ground with a loud, echoing clank.

Then, everything happened at once. There was a loud thud from the top of the stairs, and Casey disappeared as if he were never there. The door to the basement opened with a creak.

"Hello?" Theo called out as he stepped into view on the stairwell landing. He looked over his shoulder before looking back down at me. He pulled something along with him as he traversed the first step. I stared at the object he pulled. It was covered in a canvas cloth, but it looked roughly the shape of a body.

"Oh my God," I said, backing away from him. Theo grunted as he hauled the bundle down the steps. I backed into the cement wall, the cold seeping into my clothes. Once he got to the bottom step, he stood and wiped the sweat from his brow. Then bent over and pulled at a corner of the canvas, attempting to remove it.

No! I thought, even though I knew what was under there.

I couldn't look away as Theo pulled the cloth off. This time it really was Casey, and this time I could see his gray and lifeless face. There was a hole where the knife had gone in earlier. Dried blood stained his once-pristine shirt.

I was still staring at Casey's body when I saw movement from across the room. The doorknob turned, and a dark form stepped into the door frame. It filled it so completely that I couldn't see what or who was inside.

It moved closer, revealing Travis one step at a time, and I knew he wasn't alive. His clothes were covered in blood, just like Casey's. The pattern of the blood splatter matched perfectly.

"Travis?" I whispered.

He moved toward me, his lifeless eyes looking through me. I screamed and shut my eyes as he reached for me, but his hand never landed. There was the smell of smoke and the flash of flames. I backed away, running into the rough cinderblock wall. I opened my eyes, and Travis was on the ground. Underneath him, a puddle of fire burned bright blue-green flames that howled through the cracks on the cement floor. Theo stood before me, holding a lit lighter.

"No!" I screamed, falling to my knees, but the image in front of me shimmered like a mirage. A hot wind blew across my face, and I closed my eyes, but when I opened them again, Travis was gone.

I crawled forward, feeling the floor for any signs of heat, but there were none.

"We should go," Theo said, looking down at me.

"What?" I asked him incredulously. "We can't leave."

"We have to," he said. "Don't you see? This is our chance."

What was Theo talking about? He turned and started walking toward the stairs. I looked back to where Casey and Travis's bodies had been, then turned back to Theo, confused.

"Come on!" he called over his shoulder.

I took a step toward Theo and stopped.

Theo turned around slowly, letting me look at his face for the first time since he appeared. Realization washed over me. Theo wasn't talking to me. He was talking to a past Mona. He killed Casey, and Mona caught him trying to hide the body. I closed my eyes, and everything became clear. He burned Casey's body, and Mona was distraught. They ended up on the roof, and that was when she fell, and he jumped. The angry spirit wasn't Theo or Mona. It was Casey.

When I opened my eyes again, Theo was gone.

I stared at the empty basement floor for a moment. The metal box sat open, and even in the dark, I could make out a pile of ashes. Next to it was the clump of blond hair I'd dropped earlier in the night. I reached out and swept the ashes and hair into my palm. I put the hair in one of my pockets and tried to drop some ashes in the other. A loud thud came from the top of the steps. The door to the basement opened with a creak, and Theo appeared. He looked down at me and pulled something along with him as he traversed the first step. I raced up the stairs, pushing by him, and left the basement, running out to the middle of the gym floor.

Chapter 22

"Zach! Bear!" I screamed into the darkness. "Zach, where are you?"

A moment later, I heard a whisper. "Sam," Zach spoke from behind me.

I turned around and saw him standing at the bottom of the stairs, staring at me. I ran to him and into his arms. "Thank God," I said into his chest.

I felt his arms around me as he held me close. Once he let go of me, I knew something was wrong. His eyes were downcast, and he still whispered, but I couldn't hear what he was saying.

"What?" I asked. He didn't answer me.

I looked at Theo, who'd followed me out of the basement, but he wasn't watching Zach and me. He focused his attention on the mezzanine and Mona's approach.

She paused after each step. Her eyebrows slanted, and her jaw clenched. Theo met her at the bottom of the stairs, and they exchanged a few heated words, but just like with Zach, the words were muffled. I couldn't hear anything. I looked back at Zach to see if he'd heard them. His eyes were glued to the two spirits, and his expression was a mask of terror. As I glanced back at them, I wondered what he saw that I hadn't.

A loud crash echoed against the walls of the gym, and I looked back to see Mona had disappeared, but Theo still stood on the gym floor. He was motionless as he stood directly across from Zach. When I looked back at Zach, he fixed his eyes on Theo.

My hair floated all around me, and a blueish swirling light emanated from the direction of Theo. I felt a static charge in my fingertips, knowing that if I'd reach out to touch Zach, I'd see a spark of electricity.

"What is it?" I asked, expecting an answer and not getting one. "Zach," I said, concerned by his behavior. "What's going on? Talk to me. Where's Bear?" I asked.

"Gone." Zach closed his eyes, and a ripple of glowing blue light moved from the top of his head down to his feet.

I looked back at Theo, who was still echoing Zach's behavior by standing near the other end of the gym, unmoving.

I turned back to Zach, nudging his shoulder with my hand. "What do you mean, gone? Zach?" A small spark jumped from my finger to his arm, but it wasn't enough to wake him up from whatever spell he was under. I watched his chest and could see no movement. He wasn't breathing. I grabbed his wrist, placing two fingers at the base to feel for a pulse. When my eyes moved up from his neck, I flinched when I noticed his eyes were open. His head tilted downward, and his blue eyes locked with mine.

"Zach!" I said, growing more concerned by the minute. I looked back at Theo. He flickered, and when I looked back at Zach, there was a glow, and I could see the shadow of Theo's face under his flesh. They were merging, or Theo was possessing him.

Glancing over my shoulder, I saw Theo's ghost was gone, and when I turned to face Zach, his eyes were a dark inky color. "Mona?" he asked.

"No, Zach. It's me, Sam," I said, pointing to my chest. My finger brushed against a strange fabric, and when I looked down, I saw I was wearing a white dress.

"Mona, you have to help me," Zach said, but really, it was Theo who was talking through Zach. "There was an accident. Follow me. I'll show you."

I shook my head, but my feet disobeyed as they dragged across the gym floor, and suddenly we were standing down in the boiler room. The firebox was open, and Theo was showing me the flames that burned the treated woodchips.

"We have to get rid of the body," he said.

"No," I said, but it wasn't my voice. This voice was higher pitched. More delicate. "Why would you tell me this?"

"Your little games led to this. You wanted me to be jealous? You win." He spat the words at me.

"I never asked for this." The words flowed from my mouth with no help from me. We were just the instruments. Someone else was playing with us.

"You didn't have to ask for it," he said. "You just have to help cover it up. Tell everyone Casey went out of town. Tell them he was persecuted. Maybe lead them to believe that someone in town had a grudge."

My head was shaking back and forth in disagreement. This was what Mona had done.

"You have to, Mona," he said, taking my hands in his. "This is for our future."

I tried to pull my hands away, but he gripped them, grinding my knuckles together. "Please," I whimpered. "I can't." I felt myself shudder, and soon my body shook with sobs. I felt the sadness seep into my core. Mona really cared for Casey, and she felt guilty that Theo had read her journal and made assumptions. She knew it was all her fault.

"I'll tell them it was all me," I said. "He was stalking me, and I forced you to help me."

He looked at me, his eyes narrowing into slits. He touched his hands to either side of my face and tilted it up toward him. I could feel the heat coming off his skin as he bent down and pressed his lips to mine in a kiss. It was a kiss full of anger and passion.

"Okay," he said when he pulled away. "But if we're doing this, we do it right. No need to tell them you had anything to do with anything. We get rid of the body here, in the boiler room. Leave no trace."

I backed away in horror, shaking my head. "I can't. I can't." I repeated it over and over again, and images of me dragging a dead body across the gym floor flashed in my head. I pleaded with him. "Please, Theo. I'll do anything you ask, but I can't see him that way."

"I thought you were my girl. The girl that got me out of trouble."

I nodded. "I am, I swear. But this is too much for me."

He took a deep breath and stepped closer, his face inches from mine. "You trust me?"

I looked up at him with wide eyes. "You know I do." It was like I was Mona, but also seeing everything happen from an outside perspective. It was disorienting.

"Then trust me with this. Stand watch while I dispose of the body. If anyone comes, the night janitor or anyone else, distract them. Remember, I'm doing this for you."

Even though I nodded my head, my brain screamed warnings. I felt my hands shaking.

He opened the firebox and began pushing Casey into the flames.

"I'm sorry, Mona," he said, stepping back to watch the flames consume Casey. He turned around and looked at me before turning back to the firebox. "It wasn't supposed to be this way," he whispered.

I realized that all of it was my fault. The games I played. The secrets I kept. "I didn't want to hurt you," I whispered.

He looked at her for one more second, then he turned away again and let the flames swallow him up.

It was like time had stopped. I could see everything around me crystal clear, but I couldn't move or speak or even look away from the firebox where Casey had disappeared into. Even after Theo shut the door.

Theo walked by me and started for the steps, expecting me to follow him. As I stared at him, I felt revulsion. I wouldn't be able to look at him without thinking of him as a murder. I wouldn't have kids with this man. There was no future with him. And though I knew it wasn't wise, I couldn't fight the words that escaped my mouth. "I have to tell someone," I said.

His face dropped, his eyes darkening in anger. "No, you don't." He stormed toward me and grabbed my chin roughly, squeezing it between his fingers.

"I'm sorry," I said with a shake of my head. "I can't let this go."

He looked at me for a long moment before releasing my chin and dropping his arms to his side.

"I'll tell them you only helped because I asked you to," I said quickly, realizing my mistake.

He looked at me for a long moment before stepping back up to me and pressing his body against mine.

"Love is overrated," he said, looking at me dead in the eyes.

A chill shot up my spine as I looked at him. "Yes," I said, hoping he couldn't see the fear running through me. "You're right." I cried again and stepped back from him. "I'm sorry," I cried out between sobs.

He nodded his head quickly. "Casey was alive when I dragged him down to the boiler room."

"What?" I asked. I started breathing heavily as panic edged my voice. "You killed him. Here?"

"I knew you would say that," Theo said. Before I could react, he grabbed me by the hair and pulled me up the stairs. I stumbled, trying to get my footing as we walked out onto the basketball court. The floor was shiny with a fresh coat of wax. Metal bleachers sat on either side of the court, and the yellow paint on the walls was pristine and sunshine on a dour evening. We had slipped into the past, or at least my mind had. I was seeing the school as it had been that evening.

"Please, let me go. You're hurting me," I cried, trying to pry his hands from the clump of hair that felt like it was being ripped out.

Theo pulled me closer to him. "You were never good for me," he said before slamming my head onto the wooden floor. "I only gave you the time of day because you were cute. You never really had anything to offer me."

My body went limp as I crumpled to the floor, knowing that my life was about to end. I knew I had to make a sacrifice. "It's okay," I whispered to Theo as he brought me back up to his face. "I won't tell anyone."

"Yes, you will," he said simply. He threw me down onto the floor of the gymnasium.

"But I won't," I said. I looked up at him, my eyes stinging with the tears I had already shed for Casey.

Theo pulled his arm back to hit me again, and I instinctively closed my eyes. I braced myself for the blow, but it never came.

"I'm sorry, Mona." He said it so softly I could barely hear him over the din of my heartbeat thumping in my ears.

I slowly opened my eyes and Theo stood above me, his arms limp at his sides.

"What?" I asked.

"I said I'm sorry," he repeated.

He stayed where he was for a long moment before stepping forward and grabbing my arm to help me up from the floor. But when I tried to stand, I felt dizzy, like there was something wrong with my head. He pulled me across the gym floor and up the stairs to the mezzanine, and I knew where we were going.

Chapter 23

Time was malleable as we stalked through the empty hallways of the school. There were moments when I could sense the building as it was back when Mona worked here. Bright yellow paint on the walls, with artwork and projects plastered everywhere. Then my brain would flash to the present, darkness pouring in and the musty smell of mildewed walls with paint peeling off and patches of mold. I wondered how long it would be until the school collapsed in on itself?

The rusted lockers, caked in dust and years of neglect, stood like silent sentinels. Our footsteps echoed throughout that cavernous place, bouncing from wall to wall. It was hard to fathom that when this place bustled with students and teachers, these walls bounced back all their joy and sorrow.

Theo/Zach's heavy breathing brought me back from my thoughts. "I gave you everything, and you..." Theo mumbled under his breath, not ending his sentence. He hesitated, and when he looked up, I twisted in his grip and noticed that we had made it to the roof door.

"I didn't do anything, Theo," I said as he shoved me through the door. The ghostly dress fluttered against my skin in the night breeze. "Casey was just a friend." I clutched my arms, the chill chiseling at my flesh.

"I saw the way he looked at you," Theo said, his voice slurred. He pointed an angry finger in my direction. My brain whirled with the words I wanted to say, but I couldn't control what was pouring out of my mouth.

"You're acting crazy, Theo. He wasn't interested in me in that way."

"Don't call me crazy," Theo said, raising his voice. "You were keeping a secret with him. I saw it in your journal. Tell me what it is!"

"I can't tell you," I said. "And you had no right to read my journal."

"I knew you were keeping secrets from me." He grabbed me by the wrist, dragging me over to the edge of the roof. I dug my heels in to stop him, but the ballet flats on my feet had no grip, and he was too powerful.

He pushed me closer to the edge, and I covered my mouth to mask my gasp as the black expanse of night spread out in front of me. I'd forgotten how far up we were, and my knees buckled at the sight of the drop.

"Theo! Stop it," I cried. "You're hurting me!"

"Don't you see?" he snarled through gritted teeth, his grasp tightening. "I can't feel anything anymore. You did this to me."

I backed away from him until I had nowhere to go. I stared at him, knowing what was going to happen but unable to stop it. When I glanced to my right, I noticed him watching me. It was Casey, or the ghost of Casey, but he was in the body of Travis. As he gazed at me, his eyes were unblinking and cruel.

Theo/Zach grabbed me by the throat and held me over the edge of the roof. "Did you know I could push just a little harder?" He squeezed his hand, and I couldn't breathe. I gasped for air, clawing at his hand, trying to pull it back and away from my neck. I couldn't think about anything but the suffocating grip on my throat.

"Zach," I said, the words barely audible. "Please," I mouthed.

His eyes came into focus, and he stared at me like he wasn't sure how I got there. To my right, Casey came closer. He glowered, unhappy that we were ruining his reenactment.

"I think I'm going to be sick," Zach said. His face was pasty white, and his hands shook, the fear in his eyes clear.

"Zach!" I said, my voice hoarse. "You have to help me. He's going to kill me."

"What the hell are we doing up here? How did we get up here?" Zach looked around, his eyes darting. "Where's Bear?"

"Zach, let go of my throat. Please." I pried at his hands with my free hand. Zach looked down like he didn't know what he was doing.

"I can't let go," he said.

"Zach!" I said, fighting the darkness creeping inside me.

His hand slipped off my neck, and he fell forward onto his hands and knees. "I don't feel good," he said, moaning before pitching to the side.

I couldn't breathe—I gasped for air like a fish washed up on the shore. Casey was still there, but his attention shifted to Zach. He flexed his fingers as though petting an imaginary cat, and I knew what he wanted.

"Stay away from him," I said, my voice low and angry. "Don't you dare hurt him." I stepped forward, blocking Zach from Casey's view. He turned back to me, and his smile curled up into a sneer on his burned face.

"You did this. You and your games." His voice was raspy and otherworldly.

"Let us go, Casey. We didn't do this to you. Please. Let us go. I'm sorry for what happened to you."

I reached down to where I knew the pocket of my jeans would be, ignoring the dress, knowing it wasn't real. I felt the gritty texture of the contents of my pocket and curled my hand into a fist.

When I pulled it out, I opened it, so he could see the dust of his ashes, once trapped in a box in the boiler room. I reached into the other pocket and pulled out the lock of blond hair that I'd picked up from the boiler room floor. I gripped them and stepped closer to the edge.

"I'm sorry this happened to you," I said again. He opened his mouth in a menacing snarl and flicked his wrist at Zach, who struggled to get up from the roof. He was trying to control him again, like a puppet on a string.

I held my hands out over the edge. "Rest in peace, Casey Nabs. Ashes to ashes, dust to dust." As I let go, the wind swirled the dust into a blizzard, and the blanket of that other reality lifted on the wind, twirling in the middle of the ashes.

I looked back in time to see Zach rise, his eyes a blank stare. He reached out and shoved me. I felt myself lose balance, and then I was falling.

Chapter 24

I gasped, feeling the spirit of Mona Desden release her grip on my body. It was like I suffered an entire body cramp, and then everything relaxed, but it was too late to change anything because I was already plummeting over the edge. I closed my eyes, unable to stop my descent. This was it. I was going to die.

Something caught the back of my shirt, and my body swung violently as my shirt ripped at the neck, strangling me. I struggled to breathe and stared at the side of the building rushing toward me. A scream rose in the back of my throat, but it lodged in my mouth. I felt a surge of pain from my hands as I clutched at the brick wall, trying to find a handhold.

I slipped again, slowly falling toward my doom. Suddenly, a hand slammed against the brick wall, inches from my face. I reached out and grabbed it, staring into a pair of blue eyes framed by a mess of brown hair.

"Grab my hand," Zach yelled.

I reached out, terrified that he would lose his grip on the wall. I knew if that happened, there was no way I would not fall to my death.

Zach got a good grip on the wall and pulled me up with him. I gasped as he pulled me over the edge and firmly onto the roof. I lay on my stomach on the top of the building, breathing hard.

I was free to move and think at will without the prying hands of an outsider picking at my brain. I looked over to find Zach, wondering what he was thinking through this whole thing. He didn't have the same control I did, but he also wasn't connected with Theo the same as I was with Mona.

"I was afraid you were going to fall," he said, his voice filled with relief.

"I was too," I said.

I sat up, trying to get my bearings. Zach did the same, his hands still gripping the brick wall. We were both silent for a few minutes, taking in what had just happened.

Then, out of nowhere, Zach burst into laughter. I stared at him in confusion. Tears formed in Zach's eyes as he struggled to talk again. "No, I really thought I lost you." He brought his arm up, wiping it across his face to soak up the tears.

"No kidding," I replied.

Zach barked another awkward laugh and pushed himself up from the roof, extending his hand to me again.

I stared at it for a moment before placing my hand in his. He laced our fingers together and pulled me to my feet. I looked up at him and noticed a strange expression on his face.

"What?" I asked, my voice cracking. My throat was raw.

He shrugged, his eyes crinkling at the corners. "You saved my life."

I shook my head and swallowed hard, trying to ignore the tightening sensation in my throat. "Everyone needs saving at some point," I said, looking away from him toward the ground far below us.

"I'm glad I got to save you." Zach's voice was soft, and I could feel his eyes on me.

"Yeah, well—" I mumbled. I didn't know what to say in response, so I just nodded my head.

Zach seemed to take that as a sign that the moment had passed, so he let go of my hand. I felt a pang in my chest as his fingers slipped from mine. I looked up at him, ignoring the ache in my chest as I tried to imagine what he was thinking.

He looked back at me, a serious expression on his face. "You know no one is going to believe us," he said, his voice filled with pain.

My stomach twisted into knots as I realized he was right. We'd always know the truth, but no one else could.

"It's going to be difficult," he said, watching me carefully.

I took a step toward him and wrapped my arms around his waist. "I know," I whispered, burying my face in his chest and letting out an exhausted breath.

He wrapped his arms around me and held me close for a moment before stepping back.

I looked up into his eyes that studied me. "So, what now?" I asked.

He shrugged. "Now we go home."

"What about Jay? Bear?" I paused and when he didn't respond, and I nodded and turned toward the door of the building behind us. He had no answers either. I paused for a moment before looking back at him. "What if it's not safe to leave?" I asked.

He walked over to me and put his arm across my shoulders as we walked down the hall. "It's not safe for us to be here," he said, leading me to the door. "But it's not Mona or Theo or Casey I'm worried about anymore. You saw that hole in the library. This whole place could go. No one should ever stay here again."

I stared up at him and let out a deep breath, suddenly aware of how good it felt to be in his arms. He stopped, pulling me closer to him. I felt the heat of his breath hit my face, and I swallowed hard, trying not to let the tears that were forming in my eyes spill over. My heart beat faster as I struggled to keep myself under control, but the weight of everything collapsed on me. He took my hand and entwined his fingers with mine. He leaned over, his lips inches from mine.

"Everything's going to be okay," he whispered, the words dancing across my face like his breath. He placed his hand on my cheek and brushed away a stray tear that had escaped. Then his lips found mine.

I stood frozen as he gently pressed his mouth against mine. I closed my eyes and leaned into him, feeling the warmth spread through me like a drug.

For a moment, I forgot where I was. In that instant, it felt like the world had stopped spinning, and all that mattered in my life was touching him. I tried to pretend the events of the night had never happened. I let go of everything else and just kissed him back with everything in me.

After a few moments, he pulled away from me and looked into my eyes. "We should go," he said as he looked away from me. "We'll wait by the front door until they come to unlock it. When they come, we can tell them about Jay and Bear. Maybe they'll search the place and find something."

As he began walking down the steps, I reached out and took his other hand in mine, wrapping my fingers through his. He looked over at me and smiled, but his eyes were sad. I knew what he was thinking. The events of the night would remain locked in our hearts, but no one else would ever know what had happened.

He looked away, forcing himself to keep walking. I didn't know if he was afraid that if he stopped, then he wouldn't be able to leave or if it was just too painful for him to stay.

I wanted more than anything to tell him how much he meant to me and how grateful I was that he was still here.

I squeezed his hand as we walked down the second floor steps to the mezzanine. I didn't know how things could ever be normal again, but somehow, I knew that if it weren't for him, nothing would ever feel right again.

We walked down the last flight of stairs and to the door. We stood there for a moment, neither of us saying anything.

"Thank you," I whispered, taking his hand in mine once more. He leaned over and pressed his lips against my cheek.

"Once we leave here, things won't be the same," he whispered as he pulled away from me.

"They won't be anyway," I said, thinking about Jay, Travis, and Bear.

Chapter 25

We sat with our backs to the door, waiting for someone to come unlock it for us. Zach picked at his fingernails while I stared ahead, trying to imagine my world without my best friend, Jay.

"We need to look for them," I said to Zach. "They have to be here. They couldn't have just disappeared."

"It's not safe," Zach said. "Wait until we get help." What he didn't say was that if they were here and okay, they would have called out to us.

A creaking sound came from around the corner by the gym. Zach's head shot up as he turned to look at me. I shook my head. I had no energy for anything else. Then a voice called out.

"Help me." I got to my feet as Zach did the same beside me. He grabbed my hand as we took two slow steps away from the door. The voice called again, but this time it was muffled.

"Hello?" I called, my voice sounding so small.

"Hello?" The muffled sound came back, but this time it was clearer, as if the person who was speaking had moved closer to us.

We both took off at a run toward the gym, our heavy footfalls echoing through the building. We skidded to a halt at the threshold of the gym floor and looked around, waiting for the voice to call to us again.

There was a pounding on the door that led to the boiler room. "Help me." The voice called out. It was so weak and difficult to discern who it was.

I moved to step forward, and Zach put his arm out, stopping me. "What if it's a trick? What if it's Casey?"

"It can't be," I said. "He's gone."

I moved forward, leaving Zach behind, and as I approached the door, I heard a familiar voice call out weakly. "Guys, anyone, can you get me out of here?"

Zach ran forward, and we both reached down for the handle, yanking the door open. Travis stumbled out onto his hands and knees. He was covered in soot, as though he'd been rolling in ashes. He coughed, and a cloud of smoke billowed from his mouth.

"Smelly?" Zach asked, unable to stop himself from using the nickname.

Travis looked up. Confusion haunted his eyes. I wondered where he'd been, trapped down in the boiler room under the control of Casey. He'd been possessed like us, but for longer. What did he see down there? How was Casey on the roof, but Travis was down here? It made sense if Casey wanted us dead like Theo and Mona, but intended to keep Travis alive so he could use him. But for what? Then I thought about Jay being dragged away. Had that been Travis? I eyed Travis, trying not to picture him killing my friend.

"Hey, you okay?" Zach asked as he helped Travis to his feet.

Travis nodded, and I stepped forward to wrap my arms around him in a hug. I barely knew him when we entered the building, but I was relieved that he was alive. I could still feel the tightness in my chest from the fear of not knowing if he was okay. Whatever he lived through alone was probably worse than what Zach and I had been through together.

"Can we go now?" Travis asked softly, his voice a hoarse whisper.

"Did you see Jay at all?" I asked Travis, but his eyes widened with horror as though reliving a memory. When he didn't answer, Zach took the lead, turning us back in the direction of the school's entrance. I grabbed him by the arm.

"I have to go look for Jay," I said, feeling the hope swell in my chest. "If Travis is okay, Jay and Bear might be, too."

Zach put his hands on my shoulders and spoke slowly, like he was talking to a child. "Travis called out to us. We'll keep listening, but I won't let you go wandering around this place. I can't lose you too."

I wanted to argue with him. I wanted to tell him he had no say in what I chose to do, but the look in his eyes changed my mind. I could wait just a little longer to search for Jay.

We returned to the front doors, but we didn't have to wait long before the chains rattled early in the morning and the door swung open. Becca's bloated morning face greeted us with disdain.

She looked at me before looking over my shoulder, searching for the rest of us. I pushed by her, and Zach

213

followed. Travis knocked into her shoulder as he walked behind us down the few cement steps. The air was chilly. Fall had arrived, and it had brought with it the chill of death.

The sun lifted into the sky, leaving the day hazy and damp. Leaves drooped off trees like limp tongues. They were oranges and yellows, reds and browns—a cornucopia of colors placed on top of long-dead grass and bare soil. Fallen leaves covered the ground in a blanket of brown, crunching under each footstep like broken glass. They reached the end of their lives, too weak to hold on to the trees that fed them.

"Sam, where is everyone?" Becca called to us. Zach reached over and took my hand. We walked by Becca's vehicle and continued walking down the hill that the school sat on. The school slumped like a defeated beast.

The barn on the other side of the parking lot had collapsed into a pile of planks. It might have been there when we were born, or it might not have been, but either way, it was nothing more than a pile of garbage now.

We crunched through the dry leaves, snapping under our shoes like twigs. As we arrived at the nearest house, the home of Mr. Snyder, one of our teachers. We asked him to call the cops and tell them there had been an incident at the old school. He asked tons of questions, but Zach and I just sat at his kitchen table, staring down at our hands. Travis refused to come in, and he sat outside on the patio chair. I could see him through the screen door.

Eventually, after he grew tired of asking questions, Mr. Snyder got up and called the police.

We heard him talking, mumbling something about high school kids, but we paid little attention because Zach's fingers were inching closer to mine under the table.

Mr. Snyder said after hanging up the phone, "What exactly happened?" I looked up at him, giving Zach more time to let his hand inch closer.

"We were stuck," Zach said, already leaving holes in his story. I didn't interrupt. "We were trying to find our way out. We got separated from the group."

"Right," he said. "So, you have no idea what happened to them?"

"They must be hiding or something," I said. "Can you make sure they search the entire school?"

"Is there anything else you want to tell me?" he asked.

We shook our heads, "No."

"Oh," Zach said. "Tell them to be careful in the library."

Mr. Snyder put on his jacket and went out the front door to greet the emergency vehicles.

"Do you think they'll find them?" I asked, but Zach didn't answer.

Epilogue

We stood at a safe distance away from the school, watching the crane lift large sections of the building from the pile of bricks that stood on the hill. Zach held my hand as we watched them take the school apart piece by piece. There was a part of me that still hoped after a year, Bear and Jay would come limping out of that place. But I knew they were gone for good. They weren't a part of the play that Casey planned. There were only three roles, so Casey got rid of them when they got in the way. At least that's how I thought of it. I wondered how many other people or kids had fallen prey to the school. Or was it because I'd open the box and set Casey free?

Zach sighed beside me, and I knew he was thinking of the same things. Travis wasn't there with us. Supposedly, he moved to a different state to get away from all the whispers and gossip that had followed him from Littleford to Field Park. I'd hoped he'd find a place where he could be who he wanted to be. I tried to reach out to him with a number I got from his aunt, but he had yet to call me back.

The details of that night had faded, and it was difficult to remember what was real and what wasn't. Bender stuck by my side after everything, but his jealousy reminded me too much of Theo, not that he'd ever been violent with me. He looked relieved when I suggested we break up. I knew I was a different person from the one who caught his eye playing basketball in the park.

I didn't think I could play basketball that season. I didn't even want to look at Becca, but after they declared Jay missing, the team rallied together. They'd become like family to me, even Becca, who apologized for her behavior. She'd been wrapped up in the whole Bender thing, and when he started dating someone else, she had no reason to hate me anymore.

My classmates voted for Zach and me to represent the freshmen on the Winterfest Court, and that ended up being our first date. It was difficult keeping so many secrets and it made us feel isolated, but we found comfort in each other's company. I made a conscious effort to avoid thoughts of what lay ahead, instead choosing to live in the moment. I still had a long way to go before I graduated from high school. The bond we formed during the night in the school of scares was unbreakable, no matter what the future held.

About Author

Christina Hagmann is an award-winning author of young adult fantasy, horror, and suspense novels. She writes fictional page-turners that entertain and leave readers wanting more. Christina continues to lead a not-so-secret double life as an author and an English teacher. She lives in Wisconsin with her husband and their basement full of arcade games.

Field Park Horror Series

If you haven't read Faces of Fear, check it out today!

For Future Updates

Follow Christina Hagmann:

Amazon: https://www.amazon.com/Christina-Hagmann

Website: https://www.christinahagmann.com

Twitter: https://twitter.com/ChristinaHagman

IG: https://www.instagram.com/authorchristinahagmann/

Facebook: https://www.facebook.com/christinahagmannauthor/

BookBub:https://www.bookbub.com/authors/christina-hagmann

TikTok: https://www.tiktok.com/@christinahagmannauthor

9 798798 217106